THE BROKEN CROSS

THE
BROKEN
CROSS

JORDAN NEARY

Matador
Unit E2 Airfield Business Park,
Harrison Road, Market Harborough,
Leicestershire. LE16 7UL
Tel: 0116 2792299
Email: books@troubador.co.uk
Web: www.troubador.co.uk/matador
Twitter: @matadorbooks

ISBN 978 1803136 097

British Library Cataloguing in Publication Data.
A catalogue record for this book is available from the British Library.

Printed and bound in Great Britain by 4edge Limited
Typeset in 11pt Aldine401 BT by Troubador Publishing Ltd, Leicester, UK

Matador is an imprint of Troubador Publishing Ltd

FOREWORD

The Crusades are my favourite period of history, an interest ignited in me by Christopher Tyerman's book, *Gods War: A New History of the Crusades*, which provided me with the information I needed for some of the factual events of my book. After reading *The Mosaic of Shadows* by Tom Harper, a fictional character's account of the crusaders arriving at Constantinople, I decided to write a fictional account of the Crusades from the point of view of a Saxon joining up with the Duke of Normandy.

Although Cristo is wholly fictitious, I tried to be as realistic as possible and include actual events in which Cristo might play roles of varying importance. There are events I invented or altered but this was mostly where the actual facts are contested or unknown, or to add depth to Cristo's character. I intended for Cristo to act as if he was a medieval warrior with the religious outlook of a modern-day Roman Catholic – such a reconciliation was difficult in parts, but I believe it is not wholly unrealistic.

CHAPTER ONE

"It is well known that no matter how well a man shall lead his life, he shall always be a sinner! Every man, therefore, must seek absolution and remission of sins. The pope in Rome has called upon all good Christians to answer Jerusalem's call for freedom. He promises the suspension of all legal proceedings. The churches guarantee for all land holdings and the forgiveness of sins for which you repent. Men across Europe are pledging their allegiance to their lord and swearing a vow to liberate Jerusalem. I call upon all of you to join ranks with your brethren and take the cross!"

I stepped forward among the mass of bodies, head bowed, and knelt at the foot of the priest.

Immediately a cross was ripped from cloth and placed across my breast. I stood up and turned towards those still waiting and cried to them, "*Deus vult! Benedicat nos Deus in itinere!*"

The ensuing cries of *Pater Noster* overwhelmed me. An English army had never materialised, therefore I had been obliged to make my way to France, the centre of the crusading zeal, where I was overjoyed to be called to the ducal court of Robert of Normandy.

"How old are you, boy?"

"Seventeen, your lordship." My French was clumsy but passable.

Robert motioned to his side for a servant to approach me. The duke was by no means an impressive man; being short and stout, he had the nickname, Curthose. In his youth he had been an impressive and courageous military leader, but he was now forty-one and still in his younger brother's shadow.

His brother had been left the kingdom of England and instead he had inherited his father's duchy. His residence was hardly splendid either – rumours that the duke was so poor he was forced to stay in bed for lack of clothes were suddenly more believable. It was even whispered around England that in order to fund his part in the expedition, he was mortgaging the Duchy of Normandy to his brother. There were no signs of an illustrious ruler abounding around the demesne.

The servant approached, "If you are to serve his lordship, you will be expected to swear fealty unto him."

It was reassuring to hear words in Saxon for once, and though reluctant to swear fealty to a Norman, I realised how perilous my situation was. I had a choice of serving him and travelling to Jerusalem with an army for support, or riding alone. The former, though a stain on my personal honour, was the only possible option. Reluctantly, I agreed to submit to his demands. The council of Clermont and the papal call to arms had been a year prior and yet Rome was still no closer to receiving Jerusalem into its arms. Slowly, armies began to gather. Bohemond de Taranto, Robert of Flanders, Baldwin de Boulogne and Count Hugh of Vermandois all took the cross.

Months were passing and I slowly began to lose my

nerve. The crusaders were all to be Norman or Frankish; how could I possibly trust men whose language was near incomprehensible? I was looked upon with derision; the Saxons had failed to even defend their own isle, so how could Saxons be expected to safeguard Jerusalem? Many of the men who fought at the Byzantine debacle of Manzikert were Saxons, too. I could not understand their language but the song of Roland resonated in my mind throughout my stay in Normandy.

The question of financing the expedition then appeared. I had hoped by swearing fealty to Robert I could guarantee passage to the Holy Land, but, alas, Robert was a geographically convenient choice. However, it was clear he lacked the monetary resources to undertake the expedition.

Ideas were bandied around about how to raise the money. I know little of what they said but eventually the duke rose and, raising a glass I fear was more water than wine, he proclaimed, *"A mon frère, je hypothéquerai la terre!"*

My French had begun to improve so I knew what this meant. The drunkards of England spoke the truth; Normandy was to be mortgaged to William, the duke's brother – the king of England and my nominal overlord.

When the duke returned to his seat, one of his courtier's seemed to question him before glaring over at me. The duke considered the suggestion before beckoning me over. I feared the worst. *Was my adventure over before it had even begun? Was I a suspected traitor?*

When I reached the ducal seat, I knelt before him, hoping for clemency. The duke turned to me, his face betraying a hint of satisfaction with the agreement.

The courtier spoke first – it was the same as he who had

translated the oath of homage. "The duke has decided that our envoy for this mission shall be you. Fraternal relations have been... somewhat tenuous since 1088 and he hopes by sending one of his own subjects to negotiate with him, he will encounter no difficulty in obtaining the mortgage."

I took my time in digesting the words. When I regained my focus, the duke arose and I knelt in submission. He put his hand on my shoulder and spoke some words to me.

The translator took an inquisitive tone, "The duke wishes to know whether you have been knighted, Cristo?"

"For seven years, I was in the service of a local earl. He died just as I reached maturity; dejected, I returned home," I responded.

The translator interceded once more. The duke seemed disappointed, but after a short contemplation came up with a reply, then, without pause, he left the room.

I returned to my feet.

The courtier announced, "The duke says this cannot do. Tonight, Cristo, you must spend your solemn vigil in the church. The duke shall not send someone with such a low rank to conclude business with his brother. He wants you ready for a knighthood tomorrow."

He continued, "The duke says you may bathe in the Seine, if you so please."

Now, bathing in the Seine at such a late hour was not ideal, but I was left without a choice. I was, after all, obliged to bathe myself in preparation.

When I returned, I was directed to the church of St Ouen to begin the vigil. Traditionally I was to remain awake all night else I would fail and would not be knighted. I approached the altar and prostrated myself. I knew this

4

would be a rather challenging experience; for ten hours, I could do nothing more than pray.

The first two hours passed without a problem – the "Our Fathers", "Hail, Holy Queens" and "Hail Marys" becoming rhythmic. As the fourth hour began, my mind began to wander. I knew I had signed up for a religious expedition but surely such intense prayer was more befitting a monk than a warrior. I prayed that our endeavour would be successful; prayed that when we returned, it would be as triumphal heroes; prayed that I should live to see Jerusalem; prayed that the faith I should find should never lapse; that our deeds shall be sung throughout the ages. I prayed for all I could think of worthy of a prayer.

Eight hours eventually passed. I looked up and around. I was in God's house about to be knighted to save the land he had blessed with the presence of his only son on earth, but yet there was no inspiration. I was no more inspired than I was before. I contemplated this thought for what seemed like an eternity – was this a good sign? Was I so filled with fervour there was nothing left to inspire me?

Or was it that I was so devoid of devotion to the cause that even such a vigil could not lift my spirit? Would this mean I would die on the crusade? The thought tormented me but I was in luck, the courtier appeared.

"Cristo, you may end your vigil. The others shall arrive to celebrate mass soon."

*

The knighthood ceremony was shrouded in religious meaning. My clothes, especially my white vesture, represented purity. The red robe covering was a symbol of nobility. A knight's shoes and hose were black – a symbol of death. It was, after all, our vocation to fight and possibly die in defence of our Lord.

The mass was always lengthy. It was only four months since I had been at mass to take the cross and yet here was a French preacher, articulating the noble duties I was to undertake. Finally, at the conclusion, the Count of Eu, who was to act as my sponsor, took possession of the sword and shield and handed them to the duke. Now I was to be publicly presented to the Lord. I was to be handed to the duke by another two sponsors – the Baron of Avranches and the court translator had been selected for this duty – and having been presented, I was to take the knightly vows before the Lord.

The first vow was an oath of fealty to Robert. Because I had already swallowed my pride to begin my venture on crusade, and knowing that without such vows I stood no chance of success, this new oath proved less morally troublesome. The second vow was me accepting my knightly duties.

Robert began, "Do you, Cristo of the Saxons, agree to never traffic with traitors?"

"I do and I promise to chastise them for their disloyalty," I responded.

"Do you agree never to give evil counsel to a lady, whether married or not, and treat her with great respect and defend her against all?"

"I promise."

"Cristo, do you agree to observe fasts and abstinences and every day hear mass and make offering in church?"

6

"I promise so long as God shall grant me the ability to do so, I shall always honour the church." I bowed my head.

"I therefore dub thee, Sir Cristo."

As his words finished, the sponsors rushed forward to attach spurs to my feet and gird my sword. I could not bear the suspense of waiting. I was isolated at court as a foreigner and the Norman's drunken chanting was a sound comparable only to the screams of a dying ox.

*

When I finally received my orders to travel to England, I did not hesitate making preparations. I dressed in my new knightly regalia as they were, by all accounts, the finest clothes I owned. King William was a snob and I knew that whatever I wore, he would sneer at me. Hence I took care to imitate the appearance of an emissary but did not concern myself with courtly fashion.

The channel crossing was fraught with peril and I feared for my life. My first crossing was made in broad daylight and the channel was as calm as could be hoped, but this crossing was made well into the night and I felt the bite of the cold sea air before I could see the channel. Despite all of this, my fatigue caught up with me. I had not slept soundly since my knighthood and I found myself asleep with my back rested against the mast being rocked by the motions of the seas. Perhaps it was for the best; the impression made by a yawning diplomat was hardly likely to be positive.

The next thing I remember was when a crew member attempted to wake me from my repose. No sooner had he laid a hand upon my shoulder than I had grabbed his arm, ready to kill him. Luckily, I returned from my groggy state and released my grip.

"We have arrived in Pevensey, sir," he said, somewhat shocked by my reactions.

"Home," I replied. "Shame it's run by forei—"

I quickly stopped myself, realising these men were Normans and could easily leave me stranded if they took offense. However, I felt certain that Robert had arranged the landing at Pevensey in order to reinforce my subordination to him.

I felt strangely at ease as soon as I stepped back on land. I was home even if I did not desire to return yet. I still felt more comfortable. The road to Winchester was comforting in a strange manner. I knew what awaited me at the journey's end and thus I took most enjoyment from travelling.

As I arrived at Winchester, I grew weary. I was swiftly ushered into the royal court and made to wait for the king to agree to meet me. After waiting for two hours, only my thoughts prevented me from turning to lunacy.

I had been forced to abandon my sword and axe in Normandy. Robert had been prudent enough to recognise that having me enter with a weapon, even if sheathed, could be interpreted as a threat and a *casus belli* for William to wage war on his brother, most likely imprisoning me. We could not afford such a diplomatic incident delaying our departure for the Holy Land, hence my lack of arms.

Perhaps Robert had even predicted the thoughts going through my mind: if I had my sword, perhaps I could request to kiss his hand in order to approach him and when near enough, run him through. Perhaps I could even crown the etheling in his place, a Saxon king for a Saxon kingdom – but this was all just folly. I had no arms and I would have to meet the king on peaceful terms.

Finally, I was called into the throne room. I had barely passed through the doorway before William addressed me in a typically derogatory fashion, "The infamous Cristo, the Saxon who defected to the Duke of Normandy, comes here to beg for alms!"

"Ave, your lordship!" I responded, though my head thought otherwise. "I come as a servant of God to request your aid for the forthcoming crusade."

"And what is it you ask?" he asked.

I continued, "I merely beseech you for 10,000 marks as a mortgage for the Duchy of Normandy."

He sneered at this proposal. "If I wanted Normandy, I could take it at any moment. Why should I pay for the privilege?"

"Because if you agree, I can guarantee peace as long as your brother is on crusade."

"And what if he returns alive, unharmed? You expect me to simply give him the duchy back?"

"What if he does not return?" I responded. "Then you shall have the duchy as your own."

William leant back on his throne to ponder such an agreement. I couldn't help but feel nervous. My whole journey rested on his response. I had moved no closer to Jerusalem. I had somehow ended up retracing my steps and yet the journey had already three times appeared doomed.

William finally looked me in the eye and said, "I had forgotten how stubborn you could be. Very well, I agree to your demands. 10,000 marks in return for the Duchy of Normandy."

I knelt before him. "God bless you, my lord," I said, before slowly backing out of the throne room.

Now the endeavour could truly begin. Robert had the money for an army and I, a path to the Holy City.

CHAPTER TWO

The decision to set out was eventually taken in August. Our force was to link up with that of Bohemond de Taranto. The months of living among the Normans had drained my spirit, which was kept alive only by the nightly dreams of the sight of Jerusalem. The prospect of even more Normans – this time, the enslavers of southern Italy – was more than I believed I could bear. Yet even so, there was an unmistakeable aura around Bohemond, renowned for his large size, even from birth, and called the greatest general of the age, yet he was not even of comital status and his background horrified me. Still, I was impatient to catch a glimpse of him.

Night after night, I was agonised. My dreams of the Holy City were soured by the sound of thunder. I would turn to the sky and watch the clouds assume the form of Bohemond, laughing maniacally. I would then be forced to watch helplessly as his men plundered and destroyed the city, myself among them. I fretted that his mere presence would corrupt me. It was no secret Bohemond had designs on Constantinople and coveted the wealth of the Byzantine Basileus.

I worried at what lay ahead. Would this be my legacy? Cristo the Angelcynn, a man of avarice and blood lust, set off with noble intention in defence of the faith, but abandoned religion for a life of sin and hedonism? My prayers took on another meaning. I had been preparing for a possible death since I had taken the cross; now I was forced to pray for the strength to resist the urges Bohemond would impose upon me.

As our journey south continued, I became closer to the duke. I had been so wrapped up in my fear of Bohemond's motives that I had omitted to consider those of my host. As I sidled myself up to Robert, I greeted him with customary humility, "Ave!"

He glanced towards me and his stare lingered; he was observing me almost as if he sought to probe my thoughts and uncover my agenda.

Finally he relented and broke his gaze. "Good day, Sir Cristo," he responded, almost fatigued.

"Pray tell, m'lord, what is it you intend to do when we have liberated the Holy City?" I blurted out, not considering the consequences of my words.

He feigned a smile, "I do not see fit to question your motivation; in return, I ask the same." He drew my attention to the vanguard in front of us. "We are all brethren here now, Cristo, as children of God the father; let no brother accuse another of being untrue in his devotion to the cross."

Though this shamed me greatly, his tired speech indicated that my fears were true. His devotion did not mirror my own.

There was no turning back; Rouen was now a distant memory. I had crossed the Rubicon and burnt my boats spiritually and psychologically, if not yet physically.

The voyage toward Taranto did not lack duration

and, day after day, I became more and more isolated. I had spoken little with my comrades in Rouen and did not intend to change much of this during the journey. What conversations we did have were centred mainly on the Battle of Hastings and our subsequent enslavement to these Normans. I was forced to bite my tongue more than I hoped would be necessary. My only comfort was the daily mass we heard – the sign of peace was hardly sincere but was a welcome show of solidarity. I could but hope that these men would aid me as a fellow Christian, if not as a friend.

It was not until September that we eventually passed the Papal States. A few of the clerics accompanying us opted to visit Rome, but otherwise our contingent had little contact with the papacy. Finally, in early October, we reached Bari and linked up with Bohemond's forces. Bohemond was to prove a shock to me. He was of a lower rank than Duke Robert, but radiated a princely aura. He was well dressed, tall, slim and muscular, but wore an expression that seemed more suited to Duke Robert's hard life.

The differences between the northern and southern Normans were more marked than I had ever expected. I was relieved to be given some rest but more relieved that we had made progress towards the Holy City.

Bari was a beautiful city but mysterious. My venture to Normandy had been the first time I had left the kingdom and the sights in Bari were therefore entirely foreign to me. The relics of Saint Nicholas proved a spectacular renewal of my spirits after a long period of complete darkness. It also reminded me of exactly what my mission was; the relics had been recovered from Myra, formerly of the

Byzantines, now in the hands of Mahometans, and it was my duty to rescue all that was sacred in the east from these same foes.

It was not until the end of the month that the ships were finally to depart. After my pseudo-pilgrimage, I was left to wander the area. For all its exotic wonder, the language there was like nothing I had heard before and for the first time I began to seek out the company of Normans. In desperate need of activity, I began to train meticulously. I knew not what I would be faced with and if I was found lacking in combat, I could be less than weeks away from death. For all my attempts at accepting this fact, it gradually began to hit home that my life was endangered and if I could not rely on those in rank next to me, I stood no chance.

I tried to maintain a stern, fearless image, but I began to become more and more overtaken by fear. Eventually the issue became so pressing that I was forced to turn to a priest for comfort. We were to talk at length and – though I was assured that I was doing God's work and that should I die in battle against the heathens, my place in heaven would be assured – I still could not rest. I was seventeen years old and unmarried; my father was dead and I had no brothers – should I die on crusade, my family name was doomed to extinction. The fear of letting not just myself but all of my family down kept me awake much of the night and I was forced to extend my nightly prayers to compensate for my inability to sleep.

One night I began writing a letter to a distant cousin. I knew little of him and could not be sure if he would be of Saxon or Norman tongue. He was in his early forties and had spent a decade in captivity. It was unlikely he knew who I was or even cared, but if anyone could sympathise with my current predicament, it was probably him.

*

When the day to embark finally came, my sense of joy was short-lived. Both armies were to be embarked together and we were all gathered on the dock. It was impossible to estimate exactly how many men were not mustered around the area, but the number must have been at least 5000. I was thus penned in between a Norman knight, who managed to batter me with the flat side of the sword so often it became almost rhythmic, and what I, at first, believed to be a tree trunk, but turned out to be an Italian mace man.

I had often feared captivity lest I be sold as a slave; the mere thought of being chained and displayed at a slave market ran shivers down my spine. However, my current experience at the dockland exceeded all my fears and imagination. Spending hours in full chainmail unable to rest while being scorched by the sun felt like my first great trial and I was yet even to attempt to board the ship.

When we were finally shepherded towards our waiting vessel, it finally dawned on me that being so weighed down by armour meant that if I were to fall into the water, no man would have been able to save me from drowning. I admit my mind had sometimes curiously wandered onto the subject of what lay beneath the depths, but I was certainly not *that* curious about it.

As it was, my boarding was rather simple and I needn't have worried at all. Now was the time to meet the men

The crossing was no more difficult than my previous ventures and I was sufficiently resistant to the rocking of the ship to retain my balance as the waves hit. I was also fortunate to remain relatively healthy and composed during the crossing. Some of my fellow pilgrims were less fortunate and spent much of their time vomiting over the side of the ship. The ship was not especially large but was spacious enough that I was not having flashbacks to my torture on the docks.

My training was temporarily suspended not only to allay the captain's fear that we may stage a mutiny (not that any of us could have navigated our way home if cooperation had somehow become viable anyway), but also to ensure my training was not mistaken for a challenge to duel. One mistake could sour relations, which were already strained almost to breaking point.

Though I could reason that no one would have dared murder a fellow *crucesignati* in their sleep, as not only would this be cowardly and a great shame on their honour, but the spiritual and temporal sanctions for the murder of a holy knight would not have made my elimination worthwhile.

I had been rather specific in my preparations and had sought to adapt to the situations as they arose, but I found it difficult to adapt to life among the pilgrims. I found it harder and harder to bear my inability to carry even a minor conversation with them and I was forced to simply sit there as if I was a mute seeking a miraculous cure. I do not know how long it had been by the time one of them approached me. I felt like it had been a month but when I counted our communal prayers, it was probably just short of a week and a half.

He was a fairly short man and did not look like he was especially fond of fasting, for he looked rather well fed, but this was no reason to distrust him. He greeted me in an inquisitive fashion.

"You are an Angle, are you not?" He spoke in Norman French – a not reassuring reminder that Normans were an inescapable plague to me.

"I was born in the land of the King of England, if that's what you mean," I responded.

He then began to look at me almost as if he was analysing everything about me. I had, by now, discarded my armour for day-to-day pilgrim vestments, but he appeared not to be examining me for martial prowess. His inquisitive introduction made me wonder whether he had ever seen a Saxon before. This made what came next even more shocking.

"You do not speak the classical languages then?"

I was surprised not by his words, but by the fact that they were delivered in my native tongue, thus I was quite taken aback. His voice betrayed the fact that he was not a native speaker, but I found it difficult to pinpoint exactly where he had come from. I had, in fact, been educated with a basic knowledge of Latin by my guardian, but I would have made a poor scribe. However, I had no knowledge whatsoever of the Greek language, nor was I certain of his intentions in asking.

Various thoughts were running through my head. *Did he believe me to be a spy? For the Papal States, perhaps?* If so, he was certainly not the first one to accuse me of espionage or perhaps he himself was a spy. I would be well placed as a member of Duke Robert's personal contingent to acquire sensitive plans and as an Anglo-Saxon, my loyalty was probably the most questionable of all his men. So long as the rest were given their provisions on time, they would follow Robert as far as he requested them to.

I grew rather angry inside. Did this man genuinely believe I would renounce my oath of fealty to Robert and betray my Christian brothers and sisters to the Mahometan enemy (or whomsoever may have been his employers?) I would not betray my God for land or gold, and I was gravely offended that he would believe as such.

When I eventually returned to reality, I was acutely aware that I had not spoken for some minutes and had been getting progressively angrier in my expression, while he, as a result, appeared to be concerned for my sanity. "I have some proficiency in Latin but I know nothing of Greek." I quickly stated, hoping to break the silence. "Why do you ask?" I quickly added.

He gave a laugh. "I suppose you are suspicious of my motives then? Well, suspicion is exactly why I asked you in the first place." His response did little to address my confusion, but he continued, "We are to travel through Constantinople, seat of the Byzantine Greek empire and we are afraid of the agreements that will have to be made to ensure safe passage. There is no chance that us unarmed pilgrims will be allowed to even be present at the emperor's court and we fear that Bohemond will manipulate both us and the emperor. It is no great secret he has designs on the city and my instincts tell me he cares not whether it costs any of us our lives to accomplish this. He himself speaks Greek and will not be using a translator and may well seek to pit us and the Greeks against each other. I hope that if I can teach you sufficient Greek, you will be able to spread the truth of the matter and not only ensure Bohemond's intrigue is doomed to failure but also ensure that the sanctity of the endeavour is not compromised during the negotiations."

It took me quite a while to fully digest these words. He was asking me to effectively spy on the negotiations albeit for a benevolent motive. The secrecy involved was something I found strangely uneasy, but simultaneously I felt a sense of excitement and happiness. I was, after all, being tasked with safeguarding the sanctity of our endeavour, and irrespective of whether my taskmaster had the authority to give me such a mission, I felt I would be doing a lot of good. I had yet to do something important on crusade that made me feel like a real crusader, that he – whomsoever he may be – trusted that I was pious enough for this task.

Then again, he had explicitly stated that he had given me this task because I was a suspicious person – perhaps he was simply that desperate. His motives didn't matter to me, though. I felt I would be doing a lot of good and thus I was willing to accept the task anyway.

Learning Greek was a difficult challenge and I was greatly worried that I would arrive in the Greek lands unable to speak any of the language and my trial would be in vain. My teaching was, however, so intense I hoped that either we would arrive soon or else he would be satisfied that I could speak enough Greek to leave me alone.

I grew closer to him during his tutorship. We began to converse in Greek, both as a means of improving my proficiency, as well as to ensure privacy. He told me his name was Raymond and he came from the lands of the Holy Roman Emperor. He also told me he was in minor orders, an acolyte. His religious credentials were doubtless in my mind; he ensured I could pray all the basic prayers in Greek and would request that I lead our prayers in Greek. The intensive instruction proved successful and when we disembarked, I was more than capable of conversing easily in Greek.

CHAPTER THREE

Our disembarkation was no better managed than that of our embarkation and I felt it necessary to pray the night before that I would live to step foot on Greek soil. When I accomplished this, I returned to my formation and met up with Duke Robert, though after the taunts I had been forced to endure during our crossing, I chose to remain distant.

We did not have a long trip ahead to Constantinople, but our journey proved eventful. During an attempt by one of the infantry to buy some replacement shoes, an argument over price gradually escalated into a minor skirmish. For a tense few hours, it looked likely that a full-scale battle would ensue but Bohemond managed to maintain an uneasy truce between the belligerents, which allowed us to continue onwards to the seat of the empire. The emperor most likely heard of the standoff and sent an escort from the Varangian Guard, many of whom were Saxons. They provided a welcome escape from Norman company and my Greek also improved significantly in their company.

They were a rowdy group, spending a significant amount of the night competing with each other to decide both who was the bravest and who was most tolerant of ale. I often tried to escape during this part of the night, but found myself being quickly dragged back in and quizzed about my masculine identity for having shied away from the alcohol and being so inexperienced in combat. A few had not seen their homeland since the 1066 invasion and were keen to know what had changed. I was merely a child during the conqueror's reign, hence I knew little of his rule except for the stories I had heard during my childhood.

There were frequent stories circulated about the conqueror's exploits, much of which seemed to portray him as nothing short of a Satan spawn, though his descent from Robert "the devil" did him no favours in this respect.

Many of their accusations were outlandish but one such story passed around struck a nerve, that of the harrying of the north. My hometown had been one of those virtually destroyed by William's fury, and though I later realised they were merely making the same accusations of unspeakable conduct on the part of the Normans that they had previously made about other settlements, when they began to speak of places so close to my heart, it felt so believable that I began to burn with fury. I was restrained by practical circumstances in my dependence on Norman patronage, but I feared they would be less restrained in the face of Duke Robert. Such circumstances would prove a severe test of my loyalty.

Byzantium was a sight none of us could truly be prepared for; rumours of a great Christian city to the east incomparable to any we had seen could still not do justice to the awe of Constantinople. The mere sight of the walls harked me back to the *Iliad* and the impenetrable Trojan defences. At first, it appeared I would never know just what whom I was to share my quarters with. A substantial minority were unarmed pilgrims who had come from places across Christendom in the hope of protection on pilgrimage to Jerusalem; the majority, however, were the same Normans who had travelled with me until now.

Few were high-ranking knights. I was bewildered to discover that they resented me not as a foreigner but as a tool of Duke Robert. One sneered, "I suppose you were a spy in England – that is why the duke treats you so well. You've done nothing to merit knighthood!" Another quickly added, "Not only did I have to indebt myself to Jewish usurers, but I had to mortgage my lands to pay for my arms, and you just prance over to Normandy and the duke pays not only for you to be armed but pays for your transport, too – this madness is unjust!"

It had not occurred to me prior to this that the duke paying for my transport was in any way unusual. My horse was no silver stallion but would not have been an inexpensive buy. I recognised the injustice of these affairs and tried to reason with my newfound critics, but they were obstinate and I was forced to concede that so long as I was unproven in battle, there would be no love lost between myself and my comrades. The pilgrims were less hostile.

Perhaps because many were also foreigners to the Normans, with men claiming to hail from kingdoms such as Norway, Navarra and even the lands of the King of the Romans, parlay was thus a great difficulty with as many tongues spoken as mouths. However, their company was superior to that of the Normans; even if they were giving me abuse, at least it was incomprehensible to me.

was inside as the Byzantines barred the gates to us. I was concerned as to how this may affect our travels as there was a certain atmosphere of mutual distrust.

Bohemond had warned us upon our arrival that the Emperor Alexios was keen to maintain peace with the Mahometans across the Bosphorus and we could not be certain that he would not sell us over to them as slaves to maintain the status quo. Conversely, according to the Varangians, Alexios did not trust a western army inside his city walls. He had fought long and hard against Bohemond and his father to prevent them breaching his city and he was wary of them entering through the Trojan horse of friendship.

My countrymen left us early on the morning after our arrival. Ælfric, their captain, awoke me shortly before their departure. He politely told me that should I remain in the Norman ranks he could not guarantee my safety and he therefore offered to take me captive and then settle me inside the city. He was even willing to offer me a place among their ranks, assuring me that Alexios would not confine me to the dungeon if I was willing to reveal our intentions to him.

Hard as it may be to reject the company of friends in favour of the company of enemies, I owed a duty to my Lord and it was a duty I was unwilling to renounce. It was on day three that we were to receive a familiar envoy in our midst.

The envoy was none other than Hugh de Vermandois, brother to the King of Franks. As a deliberate snub, Bohemond requested that I escort him to his tent so that he could be received. Hugh had been preceded by his reputation as a shameless boaster and to send the youngest member of our entourage to greet him in place of Bohemond, as he expected, marked the contempt that Hugh was now held in by our leadership.

Hugh was dressed in foreign clothing and came with an unarmed entourage of Greeks. The smell of perfume was unmistakeable and the conclusion therefore inescapable: Hugh had taken to Greek custom and no longer resembled a Frank.

He left no lasting impression on me other than he spoke a great deal of having met the emperor as an equal and how he had been recognised as the ultimate leader of the expedition by him. Such presumptions were quickly shattered when he entered the tent. Bohemond first began by quizzing Hugh about his fraternisation with the Greeks and what concession he had gained from them. He found none of Hugh's responses satisfactory and demanded that Hugh report back to the emperor that he was willing to deal with no man save the emperor himself and it was therefore futile to send future envoys.

Hugh responded by denouncing Bohemond for insubordination and threatened him with the force of the Byzantine garrison bearing down on him should he not show respect to his superiors.

This was to prove a fatal error.

Any support Hugh may have had quickly evaporated. He was shouted down before he could add any more. Bohemond rose to his feet and in a harsh tone shouted, "So it is true then? The emperor met with the brother of the King of Franks and sent back a Greek eunuch! I owe you no fealty and nor does any man here. Return to the emperor with my message or else you may never be able to return to him alive again!"

He then motioned to the guards present to forcibly evict Hugh and his entourage and we duly obliged.

As they remounted their horses they began to converse about what they would report back to the emperor about our contingent. They spoke in Greek to hide this from us but I was able to understand. This may not have been the intention my tutor had for teaching me Greek, but it proved useful in this situation. I discovered from their chatter that Alexios was desperate to move us across the Bosphorus before there were any more arrivals, and that contingents led by Count Raymond of Toulouse and Godfrey of Bouillon had already arrived and crossed the Bosphorus. This information would have proved useful to Bohemond in his negotiations with Alexios, but to reveal that I spoke Greek would have jeopardised my chances of accompanying him on his diplomatic mission, as my tutor, Raymond, had asked, hence I was forced to maintain my silence.

Two days later, a messenger arrived and was promptly shown to the leader's tent. It was announced soon after that Alexios had accepted Bohemond's terms and they would be allowed to meet him inside his palace that evening.

Luckily, Duke Robert requested to be represented at the parley and nominated me to accompany Bohemond, reasoning that a Saxon would be a useful ally should the Varangian Guard prove obstinate. By chance, Bohemond agreed, perhaps aware that many of these men would have been veterans of campaigns he had taken part in and they would sooner kill him than welcome him.

I decided in the meantime to consult my tutor. We had not met together since our time crossing the Adriatic and I felt it necessary to consult him before I ventured inside the walls of Byzantium.

In attempting to find him, I became acutely aware that I did not know where the unarmed pilgrims had encamped. Our arrangements had been based on town and rank. I had been placed near to Duke Robert as a member of his personal retinue and had strayed little from this placing, except to meet Count Hugh. When I did eventually track him down, I found him in prayer. Daring not to interrupt, I simply stood at the tent's opening, waiting for him to finish.

It was interesting to watch him. I could not see his lips move and knew not in what tongue he was praying to the Lord in, nor could I ascertain for what favour or intention he was beseeching Him. I could not help but wonder if his prayers were united with mine; whether he was praying that he, too, would live to see the Holy City, that our endeavour would be a success and that never again would earthly desires corrupt us.

When he finished his intercessions I failed to properly announce my arrival and instead merely blurted out that I had been asked to accompany Bohemond later that evening. He jumped backwards in surprise. I know not whether it was because he was unaware of my presence or that he was just shocked that his plan had come to fruition.

When he regained his composure, we began to discuss what I should do during my time in Bohemond's company and how I could protect the sanctity of our endeavour. I knew neither Bohemond nor Alexios would appreciate a bodyguard speaking out of place and thus I could not partake directly in negotiations. However, if I could reveal any of Bohemond's attempts at subterfuge to the masses, I would hopefully be able to force his hand.

When I informed Raymond about what I had heard from Hugh, he suggested that I mention it in passing to Bohemond should the opportunity arise, but not reveal from where this news had come, instead claiming rumours were sweeping the camp.

He also advised me to be watchful of Bohemond, to ensure that he did not make us appear belligerent or threatening to the Greeks and I should therefore endeavour to give off an aura of Christian friendship instead. His final piece of advice was that I should not let the grandeur get to me; the emperor likes to give off a spectacular image and though he is doubtlessly wealthy, Byzantine military strength lies in its walls not in its troops. He would seek to intimidate us, but would be wary of provoking anything more than minor skirmishes outside the walls.

CHAPTER FOUR

When the hour came, I felt unprepared, but nothing could have put me at ease. I felt as though I was stepping over the edge of my world. Byzantium had merely been a fable to me, but it proved the most intimidating experience of my life up to that point.

The closer we came to the gate, the more imposing the walls became until I was so close it appeared they simply rose unending into the sky. We were not forced to wait outside for too long; the archers on the walls merely glared at us, uncertain whether to even acknowledge our existence. I was glad to put them behind us; one pot-shot could begin open warfare, which was the exact situation I was hoping our diplomatic mission would prevent.

As the gates swung open, a blinding light appeared in its place, which temporarily disabled me. When I opened my eyes again, I noticed I had begun to fall behind and was forced to swiftly kick my horse into action. I managed to catch back up at the end of the gatehouse. Luckily, Bohemond had not noticed me slipping behind or else I could have been scolded for failing to maintain my position in rank. The agreed protocol had been that we would be met there by the Varangian Guard and escorted to the emperor's palace.

However, we arrived before the Varangians and thus we were required to wait at the entrance to the city for our hosts.

I took this opportunity to get closer to Bohemond and release the information. "Ave, my lord, Bohemond!" I stated, raising my right hand to salute Bohemond.

He turned to give me a brief look. "Ave," he responded, before turning away.

Slightly put off, I wondered whether to even converse with him, but this information could prove vital in our negotiations and I thus felt obligated. "Rumours sweep the camp, my lord, that the Byzantine Emperor is anxious to bring us across the Bosphorus and has transported many crusaders already. Surely you must be confident you can win us safe crossing?"

He turned once more to meet my eyes. "The emperor is anxious that we are not able to amass a force that could threaten his capital – of this, there is no doubt. I had already heard that many men like us have made the crossing. The emperor would much prefer that we were anywhere save outside his walls and the further we are, the better. He is glad to see us but anxious to remove us as a threat." He then turned to look straight ahead, his eyes unmoved.

I turned to see what had caught his attention and there they were. The Varangians had finally arrived.

Ælfric, the captain, approached Bohemond to greet him. The two conversed in Greek and I was hard pressed not to react to their words and reveal my knowledge of the Greek language.

"Good day, my lord," he said.

Bohemond retorted, "Good day to you, my friend. Have your wounds healed yet?"

Ælfric feigned a smile. "Thank you for your concern. I received little more than a scratch the last time we met. I hurt myself more that day by shaving than in combat and my wound has indeed since healed."

Bohemond chuckled wryly before his face returned to a dour tone. "Diplomatic niceties aside, you were sent here to escort myself and my retinue to the palace and I believe sufficient time has now elapsed for us to set off."

Ælfric was visibly insulted and made his displeasure known under his breath. I did not catch entirely what he muttered, but it sounded like he called Bohemond "foul dog scut" in our English language. Noticeably still smarting from Bohemond's insult, he then turned towards his men and I feared they were about to set upon Bohemond. The gates had, by now, closed behind us and even if we were able to attack and defeat those in front of us, we would most likely have to battle our way through the garrison to open the gates and escape. I was thus relieved to hear him order them to get into formation around us and begin escorting us towards our destination.

Once we had been encompassed by our hosts, we began moving towards a small side street. Ælfric, who had taken up a position next to me, explained that it would be best for us to maintain a low profile, not just for our own safety but also for fear that a riot could break out if Bohemond were to pass through a crowd of his enemies. Alexios, he explained, was a realist, and though he viewed Bohemond with intense suspicion, the opportunity presented to him by Bohemond's and indeed all of our presence on crusade for weakening the Mahometans and reclaiming lost territory was more than sufficient a motivator for Alexios to abide his presence.

Ælfric then turned towards me, "Why do you fight with these men, Cristo? Why do you trust the wolves in sheep's clothing?"

It was a difficult question and one that I often asked myself, too. "Because," I responded, "I trust not them but the lamb which they serve and I have no fear living among my enemies when we are in the service of our Lord."

Ælfric showed no expression but then turned away and stated that I would eat wood. I began to laugh but to my horror I realised that Ælfric had spoken his aside in Greek and not in Saxon. He turned to me in shock. I suddenly felt the intense heat of the sun, his stare making me feel like I was being interrogated.

Had I foolishly given away the secret of my Greek proficiency? My whole mission at these negotiations hinged upon my knowledge of Greek being kept a secret.

I had hoped I would never betray a secret under torture, which made my present predicament all the more humiliating. *How could I truly believe I could hold my tongue under duress if I could not even keep a secret during normal conversation?* Ælfric broke his gaze upon me and stared forward. I could only hope and pray this meant he had failed to comprehend what had just occurred. *Perhaps I could disguise it?*

"Is there a problem, my friend?" I asked, ensuring I spoke in Saxon and not Greek.

"No, Cristo, I just... no, it is not important, forget about it."

He appeared somewhat confused. Not many people actively set out to confuse their friends but I felt a strong sense of relief and happiness that I had done so to

Ælfric nevertheless. However, I then noticed Ælfric jolt backwards, visibly taken aback by something. On instinct, I made a grab for my sword and turned to face the same direction as he.

It was Bohemond. He was staring at us, somewhat bewildered.

It was bad enough that Ælfric may have discovered I could understand Greek but it was pivotal that Bohemond did not know. I had to find out what Bohemond's plans were. If he were to discover I could understand every word he spoke, he may well have me removed from the throne room to guard the door and I would have failed. I inhaled; our whole endeavour, as well as my life, could well depend on what happened next. There was nothing I could do. If Bohemond had realised what Ælfric had not, then I could only accept whatever followed. It felt like a lifetime but Bohemond eventually broke his gaze and I was finally able to breathe again.

We were passing through some side streets in order to weave around densely populated areas, but we were still able to glimpse the beauty of the city. We had probably already covered an area larger than my hometown and yet we were still not at the imperial palace at Blachernae. I was especially interested in a sort of building that was unlike any I had ever seen.

It appeared to have crescents on the end of columns and its roofs were domed. They were not littered around the city but they were numerous. I wondered whether they were some Greek practice. *What relevance did the moon have?* I wondered. They were not especially grand feats of engineering but they were larger than any of the churches

I had seen in England and probably not much smaller than some of those I had viewed in Norman Apulia.

I turned to Ælfric and asked him what these strange buildings were called. He turned towards them nonchalantly and appeared not to notice, for he asked me numerous times which strange buildings I was referring to before I finally received an answer.

They were called mosques. I had not come across this word during my Greek lessons, but I was hardly perfect in my vocabulary – hence I was not worried about the appearance of an unknown Greek word. The people we saw were also different; the vast majority were dressed in bizarre clothing like those Hugh had been wearing. There were also many dressed in flowing robes, wearing what appeared to be cloth around their heads. Their faces were very dissimilar to mine or even Ælfric's, and were a different colour entirely. I had been shocked, at first, to see how pale I was in comparison to Ælfric despite us both being of Saxon stock, but they were a darker shade than even he. Despite all these differences, I was drawn to one similarity between many of these new people and Ælfric. They sported magnificently long beards – perhaps this was an eastern custom. Many Saxons grew moustaches, which especially helped distinguish us from the Normans, who were primarily clean-shaven, but beards were much less common back home among both Normans and Saxons alike.

Our jutting around the side streets helped prevent any conflict or unrest arising, but it did cause a sense of unease that we were being taken out of the way so that we could be made to simply disappear.

The people seemed unfazed by us and simply ignored us. Those who did take an interest seemed to be more interested in the Varangians than in us. Ælfric did not want any distractions and forced anybody who seemed to be too interested inside. As we passed a monastery, a monk found himself in our way and sprinted to avoid being trampled (the careless attitude the Varangians had shown to those who crossed their paths left me in little doubt that they would have trampled him if he had refused to move). Unfortunately, he stumbled on a rock and his habit rose over his head, revealing that the monk was wearing nought but his habit – a piece of comedy that bridged the cultural gaps and made us all laugh. One of Bohemond's guards questioned monastic practice in dress; it was not uncommon, I knew, for monks to forsake undergarments in order to keep themselves cool and better resist the heat of lust.

I, myself, slept unclothed for the very same reason, but Bohemond proposed that such a lack of clothing encouraged an imbalance of the humours as the person would thus become colder and their phlegm or black bile humours may rise to unsafe levels. Perhaps this was at fault for my recent despondency?

Finally, we arrived at the palace. Ælfric demanded that he, as Varangian leader, be allowed to enter first and thus we were forced to change our formation to accommodate this. When we entered the stable, the boys quickly rushed forwards to take our reins. One asked me if we came on behalf of the foreigners outside but I feigned ignorance. I doubted the emperor was astute enough to test our proficiencies in Greek, but I had survived one scare and was unwilling to take another risk.

Straight from this, we were lead into the atrium. Ælfric turned towards us. "It is late now," he said, "and the emperor will soon be eating his evening banquet. Negotiations will have to be postponed."

Bohemond simply responded, "So be it," though he did request to be allowed to dine at the emperor's table. His request was granted but he chose to take only one of his own personal guards as Ælfric assured him the security arrangements were sufficient.

I know not what was spoken at this impromptu meeting, as the rest of us were led into a side room to dine with Ælfric and some of his troops. We were given simple bread and wine; though this was a comparatively barren dinner, it was hugely symbolic. Our Lord had eaten bread and drunk wine among his friends at his last supper and as I began to eat, I worried my final supper would be exactly the same. The fact that he was betrayed to execution by one of his friends was not lost on me and I looked among everyone for signs of deceit. I was among both friends in Ælfric and my countrymen and enemies in the Normans. All were my brothers in Christ, but each were suspicious of the other and I was left to straddle the divide – a target for men of both loyalties.

I had deliberately chosen to eat alone in the hope that I could contemplate in private what I would do from here. Although my motive for being with Bohemond was to eavesdrop on his negotiations with the Byzantine Emperor, I would still have to be vigilant – only a poor soldier would let his guard down in a hostile city. True, I was more than willing to defend Bohemond with my life despite my personal animosity towards him, but my own life was at risk, too. Much as I hated the prospect, my own survival chances were inextricably linked with those of Bohemond, and if I was to live to see Jerusalem I would have to protect him like he was my closest friend.

My musings were, however, interrupted by one of Bohemond's bodyguards. He was not an old man, but he was a great many years older than me. His Norman was spoken almost perfectly for me to understand, as if he understood the difficulties of comprehending a foreign language. He sat directly in front of me.

"God be with you," he said to me.

"And with you," I replied.

"You are the Saxon we have been told about, are you not?" he asked.

"Indeed, I am," I responded.

Having done with such niceties, he stated firmly, "Why are you here? What brings you to this place?"

"I came on crusade to defend the Holy Land—"

"No, no, no, no!" he interrupted. "Why are you accompanying Bohemond as bodyguard? I mean, he is a Norman, the enemy of a Saxon like you. What gives you loyalty to him? When you were assigned to us, I predicted you would be a potential traitor and hand us over to the Varangians, your countrymen. Why do you stand by him so?"

I sighed. "My loyalty was to my Lord and Bohemond was certainly not He, but so long as I followed Him, I would have to follow Bohemond. My life and soul depended on it."

I expected this to perplex him, but he merely nodded in agreement.

Curious, I returned the question, "And why are you loyal to Bohemond?"

He looked away from me and towards Ælfric. "I have no loyalty to him at all," he snarled. "I serve him out of hatred of his enemy, the Byzantines. When they ran my homeland, they arrested and executed my grandfather for refusing to convert to their schismatic religion. I agreed to accompany him wherever he goes and I had no intention of renouncing this agreement when he agreed to go on crusade. I intend to pray for my grandfather's soul when I reach the Holy Sepulchre."

The Holy Sepulchre – even the mention of such a sacred place sent shivers down my spine and filled me with a sense of excitement.

We shared a lot in common. He divulged that he was from the Apulia region that was ruled by Normans and, like me, he had little affinity towards them and dealt with them as a means of reaching the Holy Land. Though our circumstances were similar, our personalities greatly differed.

I saw a lot that I detested in Bohemond in him: a lack of interest in helping our brothers in the east, a willingness to loot and pillage captured lands, and a wavering commitment to defending the ideals of the church.

He accused me of cowardice for being unwilling to kill a fellow Christian who stood in my way. I had wrestled with my conscience and found myself willing to kill an armed Christian who attacked me, but an unarmed brother was indefensible. We spent a great deal of time debating the morality of theoretical situations we may encounter on crusade. We were interrupted by Ælfric, who announced to us, through a Norman interpreter, that Bohemond was recalling us for the negotiations. As we stood up to rejoin Bohemond, I asked my companion his name.

"Alexander," was his response, "after the pope at the time of my birth."

We were led through a weaving set of corridors, which reminded me greatly of our travel through the side roads of Byzantium. They were decorated beautifully with the portraits of various emperors before Alexios and a stunning painting of the Roman Empire in the east I never believed I would get to see. The statues and busts looked like they had been made before even the birth of our Lord.

I was stunned into silence and it appeared Alexander felt much the same as he, too, spent a great deal of time admiring the surroundings.

When we arrived in the throne room, Bohemond turned towards us and ordered us to take up positions beside him. The throne room paled in comparison to the hallway we had just passed through, but was still decorated with an array of statues, including two golden leopards beside the stairs to the raised platform on which the throne sat. The room was secured by barring the door inside and Varangians were placed either side of the door as a precaution. Not even a baying mob could have broken down the door without a battering ram, and most likely, we could not have broken out either.

CHAPTER FIVE

A deafening roar echoed throughout the room. I drew my sword in fear; Alexander and the other guard did the same. We scanned the room for the threat. Bohemond was taken aback by the roar but otherwise barely flinched. The sound had come from the golden lions and was announcing the arrival of the emperor himself. It can be difficult to meet somebody who is a cult of personality; Bohemond was held in high esteem within Norman circles, but among the Greeks, Alexios was mythical.

I had read the stories of Theseus' exploits and yet Alexios appeared to surpass even him. I felt honoured to have been in his presence, but I could not afford to forget why I was here. I had to ensure the safe progression of the crusade.

Bohemond opened the exchange. "Good day, my friend," he began. "On behalf of the servants of Christ – who have pledged to liberate the Holy Lands that once He walked – currently encamped outside your walls, I beseech you to provide us with transport across the Bosphorus to aid us in our endeavour."

Alexios sat back on his throne to ponder this request. He responded assertively, "By right, many of those lands are ours as successors to the Romans. What assurances will you give me should your endeavour be successful?"

Bohemond merely responded with a question. "What assurances do you seek from us?"

Alexios laughed. "You are not a man who makes negotiations easy. My request is that all of you take an oath that so long as I aid you in your endeavour, you will hand back to me any territories that formally belonged to the empire."

"In return for this oath, you will provide us with transport?" Bohemond enquired.

"I will provide you with much more," Alexios replied. He motioned to his right. "This is Tatikios, one of my finest generals. I will send him to accompany you. He is much accustomed to the Turks and the Arabs. Without him, your chances of success are very slim. I will provide you with guides to help you navigate once you have crossed."

"What of men? Will you provide us with men to support us?" Bohemond retorted.

"Perhaps," was all Alexios responded with.

Bohemond asked for time to consider this proposal. He then turned towards us and motioned for us to gather round him. Speaking in Norman French, he stated that Alexios had demanded an oath from all the leaders to return former Byzantine property and in return he would provide them with support and ferry them across the Bosphorus. He then asked for our opinions.

Alexander piped up with a suggestion that Bohemond demand assurances of military support before agreeing to take any oath. However, I knew that our hands were tied; either we agreed to Alexios' terms or we would be forced to swim across the Bosphorus.

Bohemond concurred. "Everybody else may disagree, but there truly is no option but to submit to these terms." He motioned for us to retake our positions. "We agree, Alexios, to the terms you have set out."

Alexios smiled and stood up. "Wonderful news," he stated. "With our diplomacy concluded for the day, I will now take my leave of you. I will expect you to return for your oath in three days' time."

Smoke then appeared in front of Alexios and a loud explosion accompanied it. When the smoke cleared, Alexios had disappeared.

I was admittedly bemused by the emperor's sudden disappearance but when I saw that Bohemond was unfazed, I knew an explanation was forthcoming. Bohemond ushered us outside; Ælfric met us there to shepherd us out of the city.

Night had fallen and thus some of us were obliged to bring torches in order to light the way. It was decided that Bohemond should wear a hood in order to disguise himself. In daylight, a would-be assailant would not be difficult to catch, but at night, the risk would be much higher.

As we mounted our horses, the three of us surrounded Bohemond. He had ordered a tightly compact formation to ensure maximum security. I took the opportunity to ask Bohemond what had just happened.

Bohemond merely shrugged. "A mere puff by the emperor. He likes to have his people believe he is Hercules incarnate. He leaves in a puff of smoke to scare people into thinking he has the power of divination, but he is no demigod. He bleeds like all of us and he shall die like all of us."

Alexander shouted in agreement, sufficiently loud to arouse the attention of the Varangians around us, but not loud enough to alert anybody else in the city.

Due to the cover of darkness and the scarcity of people, we were able to pass through the public thoroughfares. As we passed through the marketplace, I could not help but notice that there were still many merchants selling their wares but relatively few buyers. Consequently, as soon as we came into view, we were accosted by merchants shouting about the high quality and rare exotic goods they could offer us. We had no time to sample their wares and merely pressed onwards. Our travel back to the walls was much less eventful than our travel towards the palace and the journey appeared longer as a result.

When we passed through the gate, Ælfric turned to face us. "The emperor has decreed that you be able to buy food in the city, but you may not bear arms. Choose your envoys and they shall be granted access to the markets."

With that, he bid us farewell and made back to the palace. We, however, continued onwards towards our camp and began to discuss what everybody would make of the agreement. If all went well, within a week we could be embarked and on our way towards Jerusalem, if it did not we could be branded as traitors and our efforts to maintain peace could be shattered.

We dispersed upon our arrival back at camp and went to bed. I prayed that night that what we had just done would be well received and that peace could be maintained with our Christian brothers. This issue dominated my thoughts throughout the night and greatly troubled my sleep, but I knew there was no turning back. *Alea iacta est!* Something would happen whether it was the result we desired or not, and it was out of my hands. There was no use worrying; all I could do was have faith in God and hope he would deliver a favourable outcome.

I fell asleep late and awoke early the next day and was thus greatly fatigued. After mass, I immediately sought out Raymond to inform him of the negotiations. He seemed greatly pleased by what I was telling him.

"He is no fool," he exclaimed. "He knows when he is beaten and this should be a cause for great celebration!"

I felt puzzled; surely, celebrations were premature. Above all, we had not yet secured passage from Alexios, but Raymond was much more optimistic.

"Bohemond has conceded that he will return any land that is Byzantine by right to the emperor. There will be no land grabbing on this crusade. God be praised for his miracle," he shouted aloud.

I was much more pessimistic. Bohemond had agreed to hand back any land that was Byzantine by right, but this would not prevent him from causing a detour just so he could capture land that was not Byzantine. I was not yet convinced that Bohemond was entirely genuine in his conviction and not motivated by land nor money. I was, however, grateful to Bohemond for making such concessions. I had swallowed my pride and swore an oath to my enemy and it is not an act one can do without a certain sense of necessity and obligation.

During my childhood, I played many games – knight and infidel, archery and conkers. However, the game that I hated most, which really made me burn with hatred, was the waiting game. It is not a game I play willingly, but one I was now forced to play as I waited for the general council to come to a decision whether to accept the emperor's terms.

Bohemond was known more for his actions than his words, but was not by any means a poor orator and though I feared that the terms may be rejected, I knew in my heart that Bohemond would succeed. None of the other leaders were especially fond of the Byzantines, but none were more hostile to them than Bohemond (Godfrey of Bouillon and his brother, Baldwin of Boulogne, had, by this time, moved across the Bosphorus).

CHAPTER SIX

In the days between the first and second meeting with the emperor, I was left to simply pass time. I made sure to visit my benefactor, Robert, each morning and evening to show my loyalty but also in the hope that he would have a task for me to make the day go quicker. Alas, he had little. He entrusted me with guard duty, but not for a significant period of time. I was a temporary solution for the afternoon guard slot.

However, my first act upon leaving my tent was to visit Raymond. Since we had been granted access to Byzantium's markets, he had taken the liberty of buying food. My paranoia had, however, got the better of me and I was unwilling to enter the gates without a weapon, hence he bought my supplies for me. I gave him the money, but the fact that he always appeared to come back with only a few coins spent indicated to me that our friendship had grown more than I had realised.

Two days after the meeting, we sat down together and during our conversation, he turned to the subject of my heritage.

"As a Saxon, Cristo, you will be proficient with a war axe, would you not?"

"Indeed, I am; in fact, I have brought a war axe that belonged to my ancestors on crusade with me."

It was still a fine weapon, but heavy and cumbersome. The Normans preferred the sword and had, in the past, jeered at me if they saw me wielding an axe. As a consequence of these two factors, I had taken to wearing my sword instead of my axe.

"You cannot wield both sword and axe simultaneously?" he asked.

"A war axe such as mine is a two-handed weapon and I would have to drop it if I were to fight using my sword," I replied.

"Then I have a present for you, my friend," he responded, before rummaging through his sack. He pulled out some kind of leather sling. "This should fit over your chainmail," he stated. "You should be able to hang your axe behind your back in this and thus be able to bring both weapons into battle with you."

I thanked him profusely for the thought behind his purchase and he merited his thanks for he refused payment for it, too. I was not certain how quickly I could change weapons in the middle of battle, but I was sure I could learn. If not, well, I could but hope my life would not depend on it.

*

As dawn fell on the night before the agreed time for a second parlay, a messenger came to me summoning me to Bohemond's tent. When I had dressed myself and arrived, I discovered Alexander already there. Our companion from the last meeting joined us and Bohemond began to address us.

"I want you to pack your things, for we are meeting Alexios again tomorrow. However, the meeting will be late and it has been arranged that Alexios will provide us with sleeping quarters. I want you to be prepared to move by evensong tomorrow."

Alexander spoke first. "My lord, are the terms not agreed already?"

"Provisionally so," he responded, "but I must ensure the specifics are in order before an agreement is made. He has promised me men and a general, true, but we have agreed we will demand 15,000 men in support for our endeavour and sufficient ships to carry us."

"What of the Varangians?" I enquired.

"I don't trust them," continued Bohemond. "I will not be asking for any of them to be in the contingent sent to us. Indeed, I will specify that none be sent to us."

"Will we need weapons?" I asked.

"Of course, you would be poor guards if you were unarmed," he responded in a somewhat derogatory fashion. "The hour is now late and you must go now."

The three of us left without saying a word. I was unsure how much I should bring with me. If I took only the essentials, then my remaining property would be exposed to thieves until my return; if, however, I took all my possessions, the bag would be almost impossible to carry.

I had yet to gain the trust of the Normans and they had yet to earn mine, hence I could not rely on them. Raymond, in contrast, was a man I honestly trusted, but was a cleric and I was not too sure how much use he would be during a burglary. I was then struck by an idea; my lord, Robert, had bodyguards other than myself and perhaps I could request for one of them to keep watch over my tent. I had guard duty early the next morning and it was as good a time as any.

It was a difficult enquiry to make. I was unsure of the protocols of asking a favour from one's own liege lord. I half wondered if I should have made a petition to him instead of asking so directly. Getting an audience with a duke, even in extraordinary times such as these, was no mean feat. I could well have been waiting days for an audience if I made a petition. No, I had to do it now or else I would never get it done.

When my replacement arrived to end my shift, I entered his tent, saying I had business with Duke Robert. Much like his throne room, his tent was thoroughly unimpressive. Indeed, other than a small size difference, I saw no great disparity between his accommodation and my own. When I entered, he was writing in his study and whether he did not notice me or whether he merely pretended, I do not know. Either way, he did not acknowledge my entry.

"My lord," I announced.

He flinched slightly before managing to compose himself. "Do you have no sense of decency? Sneaking into a man's tent and scaring him. I broke my quill in shock and my letter is awash with ink!" he shouted.

"Who, pray, was the letter to? If I may enquire, my lord?" I took a submissive tone. Though I had by means snuck inside, I had no right to be in his tent at this moment.

"To my brother, William," he answered.

"Well, then it is no great loss. A word spoken to him is a word wasted," I quipped.

Robert acknowledged my response with a shrug. "The two of us have exchanged a great many words and many have, indeed, been wasted. Nevertheless, I presume you did not come here to exchange pleasantries?"

I hesitated slightly, trying to phrase my request in the best light possible.

"Speak!" he ordered.

"Tonight, I leave with Prince Bohemond for the Byzantine Emperor," I said.

"Indeed, a great honour it is that Bohemond should allow a Saxon such as you to act as one of his bodyguards on such an important endeavour. I hope you appreciate this."

I had not seen it as such an incredible feat. "I cannot take my belongings with me and my tent will thus be left unguarded overnight."

"True," he answered.

"Therefore, I wonder whether one of your guards could be spared to prevent thieves ransacking it?"

I felt better for having gotten it out but I soon wished I had not bothered for Robert looked angered.

"Was not the horse I provided enough, or the sword or the transport? Is your presence on this crusade at mine own expense not enough of a favour for you?" he shouted, visibly furious at the suggestion.

I considered giving up there and then and apologising for wasting his time and making a hasty retreat, but perhaps it was because of my pride being dented that I opted to stand my ground. "You paid for my preparations for a reason, and both you and Bohemond trust me to guard your persons. If you are unwilling to ensure my safety, then why do you value me so?" I responded.

Robert seemed dumbfounded at me refusing to back down and looked up, slightly awestruck. "Well, the reason is we trust you," he responded, still somewhat confused. "Your zeal is not staged. We know you will not betray us for money – the same cannot be said for many others."

Robert provided me with a guard for my belongings. I took my sword and axe with me, but left my armour behind. It would have been too bulky. More importantly, a fully clad knight seen approaching the walls of the city would inevitably have been fired upon. Other than that, I brought only some gold and a theological book written in Greek that Raymond had loaned to me.

In a surprising change of affairs, Ælfric did not come to greet us. Instead, we were allowed entry into the city and expected to find our own way to the palace. I was never at ease inside the city walls when there was no Varangian escort to guide and protect us. The backstreets of Byzantium were no easy place to navigate. We could easily have been lost or ended up cornered down an alley by robbers. Right there, in that moment, I felt the sting of temptation, to abandon Bohemond and Alexander to their fate. But I could not do it. Bohemond had faith in me and I would repay his faith even if it cost me my life. I turned to Bohemond for guidance and he responded in just four words:

"*Nil desperandum auspice Deo.*"

With a slight delay to scout ahead of our movements, we arrived at the palace. We were ushered inside the throne room with such haste that I scarcely remember dismounting my horse. It appeared the emperor intended to waste no time in moving us onwards and wanted an agreement in place as soon as reasonably possible.

"Have you come to a conclusion in your acceptance of my proposals?" Alexios began. "Your proposals were very promising, but insufficient I fear. If just some minor changes are made, I will gladly oblige with our agreed oath."

"I have no time for delays. Bohemond, you agreed to these terms only three days ago and yet you come here and say I was not fair enough to you."

The emperor was right, but I could not help but wonder why he had asked if Bohemond had decided to accept them. It was almost as if he did not expect Bohemond to acquiesce so readily to the agreed conditions.

"We demand 30,000 of your own men to accompany us and act as a guarantee of your continuing support of our endeavour," said Bohemond. "This was not what we agreed!"

These words invited anger and disgust. Bohemond had specifically said 15,000 and now he was asking for double this number. I honestly could not believe it; he was playing with the terms like they were of no importance or consequence and if the emperor were to banish us from his court, we would have to hire transport from Genoa at more expense.

I understood that shrewdness in negotiations is a virtue but gambling on everything we worked so hard and suffered so much for was, in my mind, simply inexcusable. Alexios was less insulted than I was and counter-offered 12,000. Bohemond inflated this to 18,000, before a compromise of 15,000 was agreed.

With the only outstanding matter now settled, Bohemond approached Alexios' throne to swear fealty for any former Byzantine lands we may capture on crusade.

Bohemond swore on the bones of St. Paul that so long as Alexios and the Byzantines helped us proceed in our endeavour, then any lands that once belonged to the Byzantines would be returned to them.

As we returned home that night, there was a somewhat celebratory mood. We could now proceed into Seljuk land. Though things had not been especially easy, they were to become even more difficult as we would soon have to face a determined force of Muslim Seljuk Turks, who would do everything in their power to prevent us from recovering the Holy City.

CHAPTER SEVEN

In what was quickly becoming a common feature of my life, I embarked on yet another ship to cross another body of water which was only tenuously linked to my crusading vow.

It was now that we were first forced off course. In return for his continued support, it had been agreed that we would lay siege to Nicaea, a former imperial city, on behalf of Emperor Alexios. There was no link whatsoever between Nicaea and my crusading journey other than this and yet to proceed any further we were obliged to await the surrender of the Seljuk's inside. I hoped and prayed they would not take too long in doing so, but I knew I would have to endure hardship. We were unfamiliar with the architecture of the fortress and could not find an opening to exploit, hence the siege became a war of attrition – a battle of wills. They hoped we would tire of the siege and disperse. For our part, we hoped to starve them into submission. There was also the ever-present threat that reinforcements may arrive, though imperial spies reported that the local Duke Kilij Arslan was not forthcoming.

He had gone on expedition against enemies to the

east; as we could not verify this information, the fear of encirclement by reinforcements remained irrespective.

My life became monotonous in the routine of patrolling the perimeter of the blockade, accompanying scavenger parties to find supplies and escorting imperial supplies to our base. My jobs could alternate on different days but it became relatively unusual for Duke Robert to employ me as a personal bodyguard. I was not a big fan of change so, to some extent, I was relieved that my routine became relatively fixed.

Very little was happening and I began to feel too settled. It was almost as if things were about to peter out at any minute – that one day a messenger would come to tell us that the crusade was over and everybody was going home. These thoughts caused a great moral dilemma; if this were the case, should I return home? I had promised to liberate Jerusalem and anything less was a violation of a sacred obligation, but surely I could not proceed alone. I did not know how great the Muslim armies were, but I knew they were more than I could defeat on my own. I could, of course, go home and await an opportunity to return but I had endured great difficulty in getting myself this far. A second opportunity to journey east was virtually implausible! This news never came (for which I can only thank God!) but I tried not to settle myself into feeling safe.

The man who loses his vigilance in hostile territory will be the first to perish. I had grown apart from Raymond between Constantinople and Pelekanum and I was apprehensive of approaching him again for fear he would not welcome me, yet I owed him a great deal. He had been there for me when I had been most lonely and vulnerable.

Whether he welcomed me or not, I felt I had no option but to attempt to make contact with him again. He was not an easy man to find for he spent a great deal of time shut away from the outside world, studying and praying. It was a life I had much respect for, but I had grown up with a sword in my hand and a peaceful existence was too foreign for me to embrace. It took a great deal of effort to track him down, but eventually I was able to find him after mass.

My fears turned out to be unfounded as he harboured no ill feeling towards me and, indeed, embraced me with renewed vigour upon our meeting. It was a happy experience to be reunited with my closest friend and ally, as it assisted me in forgetting my current predicament and our conversations helped break the monotony. Before our departure into Anatolia, Raymond explained to me that the people there were primarily of Byzantine Greek origin, like those in Constantinople, but were ruled over by the Seljuks who were Turks.

He explained that these men were not the Saracens I had imagined we would meet. True, they were Mahometans like the Saracens, but they spoke a different tongue and shared little in common other than their religion. For me, most importantly, it was not they who had defiled Jerusalem, as a result of which I harboured no ill will against them. They were merely enemies of circumstance – a necessary enemy to defeat if we were ever to liberate Jerusalem from its oppressors.

I had not yet been called into action and I awaited combat with a combination of eagerness to put my training into practice and a realisation that my life would be on the line and there could be no room for error.

*

It was a few months into the Siege of Nicaea, around May 1097, that I believed I would receive my first experience of battle. Reports came that Kilij Arslan had sent a small force in an attempt to dislodge us from the walls of the city. Hoping to join the fight, I hurriedly put on my armour and sheathed my sword (in my haste, I forgot to bring my war axe), only to find that the skirmish had ended shortly before my arrival. This proved slightly worrying, I had been far too hasty for my own liking (what if my sword had broken or been lost?) and yet I was too slow in responding to the call to arms to join battle. I had to be quicker in real battle situations and I was gravely worried about my chances of survival.

This was to be the only major interruption to the monotony on the siege. A month later, we received news that left us first overjoyed then saddened. Overjoyed that Nicaea had surrendered and our first engagement had been successful; saddened that the defenders had surrendered not to us but to the Byzantines, who had promised them that there would be no plunder, thus denying us our right of conquest. To make matters worse, the surrender had been announced to us by the Byzantine flags suddenly flying over the parapets. It was a cold period of our relations, but one that did not yet sour relations significantly.

With Nicaea now fallen and in Byzantine possession, we moved onwards towards Jerusalem. For practical reasons, we had decided to divide the army in half and march onwards separately but sufficiently close that we could reunite if the situation demanded. One half was nominally under

Bohemond's leadership, who was to form the vanguard, and the other under the leadership of Count Raymond of Toulouse (this was the de facto situation, at least).

As part of Duke Robert's levy, I found myself in Bohemond's half of the army for the march towards Jerusalem. I was accustomed to travel by now, but I never let myself become too comfortable with this routine. I always ensured I carried both axe and sword. I could never know when they might become necessary. We had beaten back Kilij Arslan once before, but it appeared he was not leading the skirmish force and we had no way of knowing where either he, himself, or the main force were. It did not take too long to find out!

Just before we arrived at a town named Dorylaeum, after travelling perhaps forty-five miles from Nicaea, we found our path blocked by Kilij Arslan and the main Turkish cohort. We armed ourselves as quickly as possible and Bohemond ordered that all non-combatants and unarmed pilgrims form a defensive perimeter while we attacked the Turkish forces. As I prepared to join the attack, I met Raymond who was rushing to the defensive perimeter. I should have hurried to take my position, but I could not depart for battle without saying goodbye to my closest friend. We took each other by the arm and agreed that we would meet back at the camp or in heaven and we cared not which of the two it was. When I managed to mount my horse and I looked out over the assembled army, I was left in no doubt that we were outnumbered and this would not be an easy fight to win. God was behind us and thus we had no reason to fear. Bohemond ordered a charge and I went headlong into the enemy.

Alas, the Turkish archers drove us back before we could shatter their lines and we were edged back towards our camp by their arrows. Not too far from our camp, my horse was spooked by an arrow that landed nearby and threw me out of the saddle, running off in the direction of the camp. I was thankfully able to right myself, but saw a mounted Turk headed towards me, charging at full speed. There would be no way I could stop him with my sword and I could not outrun his horse on foot.

My axe, of course! I quickly grabbed my war axe from behind my head and prepared to stand my ground. As he neared, I swung at him. I heard a painful whinny; his horse fell before me and he fell with it. The fall disorientated him and, as a result, he neither flinched nor attempted to defend himself when I brought my axe down on his head, splitting his skull open. This was the first person I had ever killed in my life.

It felt like I stood there in a daze staring at his corpse slowly bleeding from the head for hours. Had it been for such a long time I would surely have been killed, hence it could not have been longer than a few minutes. When I recovered my composure I saw Alexander reach out to grab my hand. Instinctively grabbing it back he helped swing me onto the back of his horse. We dismounted close to the defensive perimeter, which I was relieved to see was complete by the time we arrived.

There was a semi-organised disarray occurring as everyone scrambled to finish the defences. Bohemond barked around orders that everyone should join up with their levies, which forced me to part from Alexander (he being part of Bohemond's levy and myself part of Robert's.)

When a defensive line had been formed, we prepared for the Turks to advance against us.

Seeing the gravity of the situation, Bohemond sent a messenger to Count Raymond, informing him that we were under attack and would need to be relieved. We did not then know where he might be or how long it would be before our relief force would arrive (should it ever be found). It was difficult seeing the messenger disappear from view; he was all the hope we had. We would imminently be surrounded and retreat was not an option. We would be easy prey and the army would most likely disintegrate should we attempt to flee. No, we would be forced to stand our ground. As he disappeared from view, I wondered if our hope of victory had disappeared, too. A man cannot control his destiny, but I was determined to do everything in my power to ensure this would not be the end.

There is very little to describe about my experience at Dorylaeum in respects to combat. We stood our ground as best we could. We could not afford to break our formation lest our defences became uncoordinated, hence we simply had to defend ourselves against wave after wave of Turks without an opportunity to press home our individual combat advantages. We fought as hard as we could – how could we not? There were no options save death or capture. We were fighting for our lives, but also for our comrades. We were determined to win victory or die in an attempt to do so.

Bohemond had sought to stiffen our resolve by passing around the message that if we remained together, we would win much booty. I didn't join this crusade for treasures and it worried me how much this stiffened the resolve of my comrades. I was forced to accept that the ends may justify the means for once. We needed any advantage we could get.

At times, my sense of powerlessness grew. The arrows continued to fly; the archers most likely hoping to goad us to break rank instead of hoping to actually kill us. It did not work; we realised the futility of such an endeavour. United together, we were strong enough to resist, but to advance would have stretched our line too thin. It would be suicide and suicide is a grave sin.

The hand-to-hand combat did not, however, make up the entire battle. Eventually, the Turks gave up the outright assault on my sector of the line (I could not see if or when this ceased on other sectors of the line) and instead simply aimed endless volleys of arrows at our positions. We were forced to play a game of patience while waiting for relief, unable to defend ourselves as the archers were well out of the range of a sword swing. I know not how many arrows were fired into my armour for I was too tired afterwards to accurately count them, but there were some knights for whom the combination of volleys of arrows and the heat of the sun almost cooking us inside our armour proved too much and they fell to their knees exhausted, completely unable to stand any longer.

However, I was soon driven on by a sound that shook me to my core. I heard a scream of agony from behind me and when I turned to see from whom it originated, I discovered the worst possible eventuality.

It was Raymond. An arrow was lodged in his chest. He stumbled around in pain, before collapsing.

What could I possibly do? I wanted so much to rush to his aid, to save his life, but I was no apothecary and could not leave my position. I could only pray for his life silently inside my head and hope the battle would not take much longer. For the rest of the battle, I heard nothing. Whether the sound of arrows flying through the air or the sound of commanders issuing their orders at top volume, I could no longer hear any of it. Instead, I heard one thing: Raymond's heavy, laboured breathing as he began to bleed from his wound. I listened for each breath, for although it pained me as much as him, so long as I could hear him, I knew he was still alive.

The battle, however, was to be a long affair. We simply stood there for many more hours, taking arrow after arrow. My armour simply became punctured by more and more arrows but I was completely unharmed.

The real issue, however, was that the sun had been unforgiving. Many more now fell, unable to withstand the barrage any longer. I suspect their fatigue derived from the heat and not from any wounds they may have sustained. It was becoming increasingly difficult for me to stand upright but I managed to maintain my position.

Raymond was receiving treatment from a monk as all this was going on. With great difficulty, they managed to dislodge the arrow from his chest and though I could barely make out the words they were speaking, I realised that they were not optimistic.

It took a long time, but none of that mattered to us when we saw men on horseback just above the hill. It was not too difficult to realise that these men were not Turks – they were far too heavily armoured. These were our reinforcements. The message had finally arrived and Raymond was leading his troops to our aid. At first, the

Turks did not see them and carried on with their assault. They were thus surprised and swiftly thrown into disarray. With the Turks distracted, we finally broke our position and overwhelmed them. It is to my eternal regret that we did not wipe them out completely that day, but we won an amazing victory and the sultan (I think that is the word these people used for their king) abandoned his camp. Bohemond's words thus came true; we did, indeed, win a great amount of booty.

My celebration was to be short-lived, for the reality soon hit home that my closest friend was still in mortal danger. I rushed back to camp, hoping, more than believing, that he would be okay. When I arrived, he was conscious but his breathing was even more laboured than it had been before. I tried to get by his side. He did not seem to be able to see me, but he realised who I was eventually and began talking to me.

"Cristo," he gasped. "What is it, my friend?"

"May the Lord God bless you in your endeavour and may he have mercy on us both. *Kyrie eleison… Christe eleison*," I responded, for I could think of nothing else to say.

He grabbed me by the hand and looked into my eyes. He seemed weak and he was gradually becoming paler. "*Pater noster qui es incaelis*," he started. "*Sanctificetur nomen tuum,*" I continued. As we prayed together, I closed my eyes, but tears began to stream down my face for which I was obliged to open my eyes. Though I tried my hardest not to look directly at him, as I was afraid of what I may see, I heard him say, "It is finished, *alea iacta est*, thy will be done." After which his hand went cold and limp.

I had never felt a dead body before. My father had died when I was young, but I had not been present when he died. I had not touched the men I had killed in battle. It was a sombre experience and sadly one which was to stay with me for the rest of my life.

Not knowing what to do, I simply stayed by his side pondering my next steps. He had been my guide through the darkest hours of my journey and now I was to be alone once more. I felt selfish for thinking of myself and not the fact he had a family back home, or that he, I was certain, was now resting in eternal peace and happiness with the Lord our God. The pain I was feeling was inevitable and there was little I could do about it.

When I eventually decided to act, I picked up his body and carried it to a priest, who said some prayers over the body before it was buried in one of the graves prepared for the dead. Seeing him disappear beneath the ground merely emphasised the fact he was now gone from me forever and at that moment I began to cry and fell to my knees and prostrated myself before his grave. Lamenting the loss of my closest friend, when I returned to my feet I felt a hand on my shoulder. I was too numb to respond and did not react.

A voice said, "Weep not for the pious dead, instead weep for those living in sin who have turned from God, for this man does not need your compassion, but the sinner must be brought back to God's everlasting love."

I did not think much about these words or who had spoken them, but I later discovered that it had been the papal representative Adhemar of Le Puy and these were words that I was mindful of for the rest of my life.

CHAPTER EIGHT

The death of Raymond had been a terrible blow to me. I had become accustomed to his friendship and advice, and with him now gone, I began to feel there was nobody to whom I could turn. I had made no close friends among the rest of the army.

I felt like this for about a month, but I slowly got over my heartbreak. The rest of the troops in Robert's contingent seemed to have a begrudged respect for me after my exploits in battle at Dorylaeum. They began to treat me as their equal instead of their inferior and thus I was less alone among them than I had been before.

I would meet with Alexander when the opportunity presented itself. However, though I got over my crippling isolation, neither Alexander nor the rest of the friends I gradually made were able to replace Raymond. I was to suffer another two tragedies soon afterwards. Firstly, my horse died of what I suspect was heat exhaustion and due to a severe shortage of horses, I was forced to make do with a cow we had captured in Sultan Kilij Arslan's camp. A cow is not an especially comfortable animal to ride and I had severe issues in using it as a beast of burden in carrying my equipment (although I was provided with a source of milk, if I so wished). However, it carried me to my destinations and I was thus thankful for it.

The second tragedy was Baldwin of Boulogne. Seduced by power, he diverted his troops towards a place known as Edessa. I would later discover that he had captured the city and that many of our supplies were provided by him using his new realm.

I am thus unsure of how to feel about Baldwin's diversion; ultimately he helped us in our crusading endeavour, but by the same token he reneged on his crusading vow. Although he would later fulfil his vow to visit Jerusalem, he had abandoned us and would no longer fight with us. I had come to appreciate the help he gave us, but when I first found out he had left us, all I could feel was rage that one of our leaders had turned his back on us.

I had expected that we would be harried on our travels from thence onwards and I was correct to think so. I had thus expected to have to be on my guard at all times as it would be an eventful trek. I was, once again, correct, though not in the manner I was anticipating. One day, I was walking alongside Alexander in a forest and we were discussing how we were faring in our enterprise. We discussed the conditions in our respective camps. He was content to be part of Bohemond's contingent and painted a picture of a caring lord rather than the beastly avaricious brute that I had heard rumours of.

I described how Robert was not an impressively rich man but was brave and kind to us all, and I would prefer him as my overlord to his brother, William. A suggestion which, Alexander rightly pointed out, was a submission to Norman rule over England – a fact I was unhappy with, but it made me realise that the Normans had gradually grown on me. I no longer thought of them as evil oppressors of my people, but as my comrades and brothers in Christ Jesus our Lord, and though it would have shocked my past self, some had even become my friends.

Alexander also voiced his contentment at meeting his Christian brethren from across the seas. I had never given thought that I would meet men from across all of Christendom. Some, like myself, had travelled many miles to join this endeavour from places such as Sweden, Navarre and Croatia. It was heartwarming that all of us, despite our many secular lieges, had been united by our love of our one spiritual Lord and were all willing to risk our lives for his sake.

We came to an open space with a couple of stumps and chose to sit down to continue our conversation, I turned to Alexander and asked him how the experiences had changed his outlook on life. He responded that he felt no different.

I should have realised that, unlike myself, Alexander had taken part in combat before. He knew the feeling to kill one's enemy and the thrill of victory and had done for a long time. My experiences had changed me and yet Alexander was still the same man that he had always been. Vanquishing one's foes was merely quotidian for him.

I felt that despite what I had been through, I had not yet accomplished anything of note. This brought me great disappointment but I did my best to hide it from Alexander. A silence neither of us were capable of breaking came over us. I had nothing to say for I was now too saddened to continue with the conversation and Alexander seemed disconcerted by the turn the conversation had taken. As it turned out, the silence was to prove extremely beneficial, as the lack of conversation made things much more audible.

We heard a scream and the shouted words "Help me!" in Frankish, coming from further in the forest. We did not recognise the voice, but we knew that whomsoever it was would be one of our own men. If, in the worst-case scenario, it was the portent for another attack by the Turks or the Saracens, we needed to warn the others or, at the very least, grab our weapons and return to camp to take up our defensive positions. When we reached the source of the cry, we discovered a wounded Frank who had been savaged by a bear. His wounds were, as yet, superficial and not fatal.

Both myself and Alexander were shocked at this and were forced to act quickly, but the bear was surprisingly sturdy and it took many blows to bring him down. Matters were complicated by the fact that neither of us were wearing armour and thus we had to be cautious about approaching the bear in order to ensure that he would not maul us. Eventually, however, I was able to dodge the bear's advance and strike at his leg. With the beast temporarily incapacitated, both myself and Alexander were able to plunge our swords into his hide.

The bear went limp and we knew we were safe. Our attention turned to the man who had been wounded. He had been seeking to flee, but it appeared that his wounds had weakened him severely for he was struggling to walk and wailing in pain. When we caught up with him, Alexander realised that it was none other than Godfrey of Bouillon, brother to Baldwin and one of the foremost leaders of our crusade.

Alexander realised the importance of getting him swiftly to safety. He grabbed his arm to steady him and motioned for me to prop up Godfrey from his other side. Though I was afraid of what would happen if we were to encounter more bears (for none of us would have been prepared to defend ourselves at a moment's notice), I obliged.

By God's grace, we were able to pass through the forest and back to camp without any incident and bring him to one of the physicians, who put aside the rest of his business to treat Godfrey. A messenger was sent to Godfrey's personal physician to summon his aid and we took this as our opportunity to leave. We could do no more for Godfrey. We knew nothing of treating the wounded and so our continued presence would have brought no benefit. We parted as soon as we left the tent in order to return to our own quarters.

I tried to settle down to pray but the events in the forest had given me a rush of adrenaline that I found extremely difficult to get over. I couldn't concentrate and felt guilty that I had been distracted during prayer. Getting to sleep was even more difficult, for I found myself laying wide awake, unable to calm myself.

When I was but a small child, my mother taught me that when I could not sleep, I should pray inside my mind until I slowly drifted off. This was not advice I usually took, for it rarely proved useful to me. I found myself focused on my prayers and it heightened my alertness. There was only so much I felt necessary to pray about. I got little sleep that night and I thought myself thoroughly blessed that I had no important matters to attend to the next day for I would certainly be too fatigued to be of much use.

When I woke up, I discovered that I had overslept by a significant number of hours. I would probably have slept even longer had not Alexander awakened me by entering my tent. He did not mean to, but he accidentally kicked me and, as a result, we were both thoroughly startled. In my youth, my father had told me legends of Hereward the Wake, who had rebelled against the Normans and slept beside his bed so that any would-be assassins would wake him when attempting to kill him. I adopted this practice, not due to an inflated sense of self-importance, but out of the belief that I must always be mindful and prepared if I was ever to survive long enough to become a man.

When we composed ourselves, Alexander told me it was now past breakfast. He said Robert had feared me lost or dead and had requested him (for Alexander knew me best) to investigate.

Robert chastised me for my laziness when I arrived in his presence, but praised me for my resourcefulness the previous night and told me Godfrey was shaken but would survive.

When I met up with Alexander once more, I asked him how, unlike myself, he had been able to sleep after the previous night's events. His response was that his night had fared worse than my own for he had, indeed, not slept at all and was hoping to slip away to rest that afternoon. Alexander did not have the look of a man beset by fatigue, but his movements and reactions were, indeed, noticeably slower than before. Perhaps this was not the first night Alexander had been forced to go without sleep on a campaign! I was thus glad of the little sleep I had gotten, for it helped me remain acceptably alert and it saved me the shame of potentially falling asleep during mass.

When mass was over, I decided to visit Godfrey to see for myself his condition. The readings of the day had been about charity and I felt it fitting to check on his welfare. When I arrived at Godfrey's tent, he was propped up on a bed with a physician tending to his wounds. He recognised me almost instantly and began questioning me about my name and origins.

"You are from a place called Scafeld, Cristo? I have never heard of this place – where is it?"

"It is between Mercia and Northumbria in England," I responded, not certain how much he knew about my homeland. "It is a small village in the north."

"What of your family? Are they also from this village?" he asked.

"My family have lived in that area for many years," I responded, curtly.

He seemed not to take offence at my tone. It was not befitting for me to address my superior in such a way, but I was also unwilling to make apologies unless he took offence. He ended by requesting I pass on his thanks to Alexander for helping him the previous night. I reminded him that we were only doing our duty even though he was not our commander and that we would do the same for anyone who had been in a similar predicament.

Godfrey smiled wryly. "Even a Saracen?" he asked.

That question stopped me in my tracks. I did not know what to say, for Saracens must surely be children of God and therefore I must be obliged to help them if in need. However, as Mahometans, they follow a different religion to our own and do not give due reverence to Jesus Christ our Lord (though I do not know how or to what they offer their prayers). This question caused me moral anguish; I supposed that a dead Saracen, unlike a living one, could not convert to the one true faith and thus I would have helped a Saracen in the same predicament. I dared not say this to Godfrey, lest he doubt my sincerity in going on crusade.

Instead, I responded, "It was you I saved last night, not a Saracen."

I took my leave at this point and returned to my own quarters once more and decided to settle down for bed earlier to compensate for my lack of sleep. I thanked God that Godfrey had survived the ordeal of the night before and our leadership was still intact.

*

I cannot know God's will nor his purpose, but the Lord soon proved that my celebration of Godfrey's survival had been too hasty. A few weeks later, I was woken in the night by none other than Duke Robert, who bade me to dress quickly for there was an urgent matter to address and he wanted me to accompany him.

I dressed as quickly as possible, not knowing what to bring or what to leave behind. As a result, I was wearing only basic armour. Robert guided me towards another tent. I found it strange that he had not awoken his bodyguards, but was guarded solely by myself. Surely, if the matter was so urgent, he would need all the protection he could get.

When we entered the tent, I saw a mass of people crowded around a bed. At first, I could not see who was lying inside, but when Robert managed to push himself bedside, I pushed next to him and discovered an old man – probably in his fifties or sixties – looking extremely ill.

He was well dressed in a manner one would not associate with bed clothes, but instead with courtly attire. It was thus none too difficult to realise that this man was Raymond of Toulouse – arguably the richest and most eminent man on our crusade.

A priest approached the other side of the bed and anointed him with oil. This was a fateful sign. He then administered extreme unction and I was hit by the realisation that these men had come to see the end of Raymond's life. Bohemond quietly asked the priest to suspend the sacrament temporarily and approached Raymond's side.

"Monsieur Raymond," he said, quietly, "we need assurances that you will appoint a leader to succeed you on crusade. We cannot afford your forces to disband."

Raymond turned to face him slowly and painstakingly. He said, "My men will probably return home to ensure a smooth succession in Toulouse. Even if I order otherwise, I doubt they will obey once I am gone."

Bohemond arose with a face that betrayed his anger. "Then we will force them to stand by us. If they will not agree peacefully, we will impose our will by force!"

Godfrey quickly cut in, "It would do us no good. If we do battle with them, we will only destroy ourselves. It will give us no benefit to slaughter our allies – and what of our own losses? No, if we cannot compel them to stay behind peacefully, then we will have to allow them to leave. We cannot go to war with our own allies, Bohemond. We will surely incur God's wrath if we do."

Bohemond gave a sigh. "I see," he said, before turning back to Raymond. "We desire you to make plans to appoint a new leader from your contingent for after your death and if he will not continue on with us, then we will let him leave peacefully."

"Good," Raymond said, softly.

The priest then requested to continue administering the sacrament. Bohemond obliged and the priest finished his anointing with oil, then turned to address us.

"I wish to hear this man's confession, therefore I beg you all to take leave for the night and return on the morrow."

We all obliged and began to exit the tent. As we left, I requested to talk with Duke Robert. I asked his explanation for why he had called on me to accompany him.

"Because you are trustworthy," he said. "I know why you are here and that you will defend me to your last breath. The others are loyal but I cannot be certain that they have the zeal for our crusade and will see it through. However, I know I can trust you to do all in your power to help us."

"Thank you, my lord," I said, bowing to him.

"There's more," he said. "Bohemond was impressed by your fortitude in battle at Dorylaeum and Godfrey speaks very highly of your bravery in tackling the bear. Your presence around me gives me a silent but powerful authority among the rest of the leadership. Many see me as their lesser not their equal."

I pondered this before responding, "I am glad to be of service, my lord."

With that, we bade each other farewell and I returned to my quarters. This time, there was no rush of adrenaline, but I nevertheless found myself unable to turn my thoughts away from the possibility that Raymond's contingent would abandon us upon his death. Baldwin's departure had been a loss but a bearable one. Raymond, however, was the very core of our army; it was, indeed, he who had rescued us at Dorylaeum. Despite all the praise we had received for holding steady, I knew well that had Raymond's relief force not arrived, we would have been gradually overwhelmed and defeated.

There was nothing that I could do, however. The question of whether we would lose another part of the army or not would have to be settled by greater men than myself and I would have to accept whatever came of it.

The next few days were tense. News would be passed around that Raymond had died, before an official announcement declared that he was very much alive. Whispers went around camp that plans had already been made for the men to return to Toulouse, while other men could be heard whispering that they had pledged to honour their crusading vow and would stay with us until the bitter end.

A scurrilous rumour that Raymond was being punished by God for having lain with the wife of the Turkish sultan also surfaced (I refused to believe this rumour for two reasons. Firstly, I was reliably informed that the Mahometans practised polygamy. The sultan had many wives and none of the men were capable of specifying which wife Raymond had allegedly laid with. Secondly, Raymond had the reputation as a great Christian knight, which I found hard to reconcile with the sort of person who would have done such a deed).

Matters were tense for a long period. Rumours that Raymond had made a full recovery continued. At first, I took no notice, for many of the men were willing to invent any lie just to boost morale. Soon, however, more and more were circulating this rumour and men of good standing were among this group. Eventually, I received the truth not by word of mouth but by sight. I saw Raymond atop his horse once more (my cow was still holding steady), ready to lead his troops onwards. There was to be no desertion of his forces. He would be with us to come before God, or to come to the lands his feet had touched.

CHAPTER NINE

In a moment of solitude, I decided to write a letter to my cousin. He had responded to my previous epistle with word that he had recovered his lands the year before my departure and had held his own against the forces of King William II, but had received reports that the same king would return imminently.

His letter was in Saxon, though it appeared he had not written it himself for he warned me that he did not speak the Saxon language, but would be able to converse in the language of our ancestors if we desired (during childhood, my family had spoken Saxon while his family had preserved the ancestral tongue. I had picked up little of this language then and did not wish to humiliate myself). I thought about my letter for a while; above all, I was addressing an elder and I should give him due respect.

I wished to be polite but formal as we were not closely related and I had never, until now, corresponded with him. Indeed, I had only heard of him from my father who had mentioned how far our ancestors had spread across Britain and how powerful we had been. I ended the letter by saying I would pray for his success and would remember him if I should ever set foot in the Holy Sepulchre.

I always found repeating myself an annoying and superfluous endeavour and hence I see no reason to discuss any more of what happened before we reached Antioch, for it was a daily grind of patrolling the camp, the occasional sortie with a scavenging party and defending against Mahometan attacks. These would continue to happen so long as we were travelling and hostile forces were nearby.

There were not attacks every day, but it was always a possibility and there was no time to rest. I suspect the Turks were waiting for us to let our guard down and then would attempt to wipe us out. We had to be forever vigilant.

Marching was already an arduous task on my uncomfortable cow and I often ached when I dismounted (I eventually named her Boeða). I was thus often tired from simply moving forward and this compounded my fatigue from having to always be on my guard and ready at a moment's notice. I didn't mind having to fight, as the role of a knight is to be a man of war, defending the men who work and the men who pray.

However I wasn't prepared for such tiring work and it was difficult to adjust to the hours. It was tempting not to attend mass every day and to sleep instead. I sometimes considered doing so, but I had vowed to attend and it was part of the obligations of a knight. If I was going to be a knight, I felt I might as well be an honourable and obedient one.

Eventually, when we reached Antioch, we were able to encamp outside the city and no longer needed to travel, so I was thus much less fatigued. However we were resisted in our attempts to seize the city and were obliged to lay siege. The news we received was invariably negative; the garrison had expected our arrival and had sent messengers to Kerbogha of Mosul, Ridwan of Aleppo and Duqaq of Damascus requesting to be relieved. This was a grim prospect.

We could not afford to wait outside the walls for we risked being trapped between the relief forces (if our informants were to be believed, any of them could call upon an army larger than our own) and the formidable walls of Antioch. If encircled and outnumbered, we would need a miracle in order to survive.

We attempted to prepare for an attack on the city and scavenged for supplies in the area around Antioch. However, after a few months, the garrison brought the battle to us and sought to dislodge us from the walls. The sortie was, fortunately, a failure, but unfortunately did not leave us in any better a position to capture the city. The lack of a conclusive or beneficial result from the skirmish left me feeling like the battle had, in fact, been a defeat for we had not captured any supplies, which had been running low, and we were no closer to capturing the city. In my opinion, this made the losses we suffered all the more painful. Reports soon surfaced that Duqaq of Damscus had answered the call to arms and would imminently arrive to meet us.

The informants stated that the full force of Damascus had not been summoned and his troops were not numerous enough to encircle us. We would thus be able to meet his army head-on without fear of being trapped. Unconfirmed reports that Ridwan and Kerbogha were also preparing to relieve Antioch surfaced, but the reports all agreed that they were not yet ready to march and we would have a few months to prepare before they arrived.

The forces of Duqaq arrived only two days after the failed sortie. We were prepared and still numerous and the relief force was beaten back and driven off. We, that is Robert's contingent, had been in the vanguard and the first to engage Duqaq.

We mauled all those in our way, but our casualties were too heavy and we were forced to turn back and abandon our foraging mission. This was compounded by the fact we captured very little supplies from Duqaq. The arrival of the new year was therefore a sombre one; supplies were running lower and lower, with little possibility of replenishment. We would need to capture the city in order to replenish our supplies adequately and we could not know when an opportunity to do so might arrive.

The year 1098 began with an air of pessimism. Things had been bad before but 1097 had dawned on a more optimistic note. On the fifth day after the birth of our Lord and Saviour, or the feast of Saint Liberius of Ravenna, the earth shook and a hole appeared in the sky for the next few weeks. Many of the preachers took this as a sign that God was commanding us to cease our pillaging lest he wreak vengeance upon us.

Adhemar commanded us to obey a three-day penitential fast. I happily obliged, not that there was much food to go around anyway. I did not, however, feel this was divine judgement for our sins, as during this time Duqaq retreated from Antioch and returned to Damascus and would not harm us further during the siege.

We weren't sure how much longer the garrison could hold the city, but neither did we know how much longer we could survive without more supplies. Some nearby

Christians sold us some food, but the desire for money burned brighter in their hearts than the spirit of Christian brotherhood and we could thus not afford a great deal. How these men could call themselves Christians while watching their brothers die of starvation was an abomination to me.

All the rest of January was spent hoping that there would soon be a breakthrough, but there was no such joy. Indeed, we received ill tidings instead. Ridwan had apparently outfitted his army quicker than we had estimated and would soon be upon us. Many men were panicking but Bohemond showed his exceptional leadership quality, as he had done at Dorylaeum, by assuring us that so long as we were steadfast in holding the line, we would never be defeated.

Some knights did desert; some came back again. The most high-profile desertion was that of Peter the Hermit, a peasant preacher who had lead a crusade of the peasantry before we arrived. Bohemond sent some men after him and he was eventually pardoned.

*

One night, when I was struggling to sleep, I took a walk around the camp and discovered Bohemond discussing matters with Tatikios. Tatikios had fire in his voice and I ducked behind a nearby wagon to listen in on them. Greek was, by now, second nature to me and I had no trouble in translating their words. Tatikios was expressing anger at being ignored by the leaders, including Bohemond. He said that if we were running low on supplies, then we should prosecute the siege from a distance so as to minimise the risk of a sortie and allow a greater scavenging range. He emphasised how he was advising us in good will and for our benefit and yet was continually ignored.

Bohemond listened to his complaints before saying that the other leaders were suspicious of Tatikios, and rumours had even abounded that he was in league with the Turks and that Tatikios already had a price on his head.

I had never heard Robert mention such accusations, though they had been passed around some of the pilgrims. I suspect, however, that Bohemond was not being wholly truthful. Tatikios was taken aback by this and was dumbstruck. Bohemond advised him to make himself scarce, as if he remained he would not be long of this world. Visibly still in shock, Tatikios walked away without saying a word, mounted his nearby horse and set off back the way we had travelled. I was shocked at what had just happened.

Was Bohemond telling the truth? Surely not, but then again I would not have been informed if it were true and Robert would never have revealed it to me if I asked. There would be no way for me to verify this information. I waited for Bohemond to leave and left my hiding spot to return to my room, still unsure what to make of what I had seen.

Soon after we awoke the next morning, we were called together to hear Bohemond speak. He announced to us that Tatikios had fled from our camp and would not be returning. He continued:

"The Greek expressed fear of the advancing Saracens. He believed we would not be able to defeat them as they have defeated the Byzantines many times. The man is a coward and we owe nothing to these effeminate and cowardly Greeks. While we fight and die for our Lord, they hide behind our defences and plot to save their sorry skin. We all know that Tatikios was secretly in contact with the Saracens and ready to sell us out for their gold. We should be glad to be rid of this wretch. Let us celebrate our freedom from the tyranny of the Greeks."

I held my tongue, though I knew Bohemond was lying. Tatikios had left our camp fearing for his life. He was no coward – he had advised us as best he could even at the end. He had never hesitated to join us in our battles.

As we left, I managed to speak to Alexander. He expressed his satisfaction that Tatikios had left the camp and would not be returning and then he said something that put everything into perspective, "I suppose since Tatikios has abandoned us, the emperor has reneged on his promise to support us."

I did not believe that we had been abandoned, but in order to be courteous, I agreed with his suggestion. "I suppose we no longer need to be bound by oath to give the emperor the lands he used to own."

It then finally hit me. Bohemond wanted rid of Tatikios, so he could claim Antioch for himself. It had not been too long since it had been a Byzantine city, and by portraying Tatikios and the emperor as reneging on the agreement, he could justify his refusal to honour it by arguing they had already broken it.

When news later reached us that Ridwan's army was soon to arrive, Bohemond played this to his advantage, stating that unless it was agreed that he could have Antioch as his own private fief, he would take no further action in our military campaign.

The word for this, I am sure, is extortion and it was

a threat that none of the other leaders wanted to happen. Godfrey and Raymond of Toulouse resisted this suggestion and refused to agree, but the infantry and minor knights were sympathetic to Bohemond's cause – no doubt out of respect for his martial prowess.

I was disgusted that Bohemond had the bravado to make such a threat, but I doubted his sincerity in making it and I was proved correct as he did not desert. Bohemond was an enigma, capable of manipulating matters to suit his own cause and though it made him thoroughly devious, it also inspired some begrudging respect for his diplomatic ability. He always seemed to get what he wanted and this could serve us well in future negotiations.

CHAPTER TEN

Ridwan's forces were first spotted just before the Feast of Saint Ansbert of Rouen. All our cavalry was sent out to meet them, though as I was without a horse, I was not one of them. We were to meet them in full battle in order to prevent them crossing the Iron Bridge. We charged at them and though they suffered a few casualties, we were eventually forced to continue battle in a narrow pass. This suited us better as we were able to use the river and lake to protect our flanks, thus preventing Ridwan from putting his superior numbers to good use.

After some heroic defending, we charged once more and the Mahometans scattered and fled the field in disarray. On our return, we discovered that the garrison had sallied out to break the siege, hoping to use the battle as a distraction. The tactic almost worked as they had pushed those who had not joined the battle back from the walls. With our return, they were forced to retreat to the city or face a massacre. Further good news was relayed to us; during his march, Ridwan had captured a nearby city called Harim, but when we routed his army, the garrison had abandoned the town in fear and we recaptured it without a fight.

There was, however, a surprise in store. Edgar the Ætheling, the last of the Cerdic line and rightful King of England, arrived by ship, carrying supplies from Emperor Alexios. He was nominally the leader but only as a result of his royal blood. He owned no land and held no lordship that he could call his own, as a result some of those with him were theoretically more powerful than he despite his royal lineage.

A fierce battle broke out after their arrival as the garrison sallied forth once more. It was even rumoured that both Raymond and Bohemond had been killed defending them. Command fell to Godfrey, who feared that the escort would be massacred. I was only moments away from being sent with Duke Robert to rescue any survivors when the remnants of the garrison set upon us and we were forced to hold our position as best we could. Although we managed to resolutely stand fast, we urgently needed reinforcements. After dogged resistance, Bohemond and Raymond arrived to turn the tide of battle. Up until this point, the defenders had been able to swiftly retreat back behind their walls.

However, we managed to organise ourselves more quickly than they did and, as a result, over one thousand Mahometans perished trying to return. With the battle now won, we were able to make use of the supplies we had been brought. We had received enough material to construct both siege engines and a fort that was under Raymond's command. We named it La Mahomerie; it blocked the bridge gate and protected our supply route from attack. Tancred of Lecce, who was Bohemond's nephew, also garrisoned a nearby abandoned monastery.

When I finally came face to face with Edgar, I knelt

before him as my right and true lord. However, he told me to return to my feet as he held no title with which to lord over me. He explained that he had given up hope of regaining the crown of England, though technically he had never been crowned in the first place, and was content to simply become a man by gaining a fief of his own. He was as old as my lord, Robert, for they had been born in the same year but Edgar was much more impressive.

He spoke my English tongue, was taller, better dressed and had an air of authority that Robert often lacked. We conversed about affairs back at home during my absence. Edgar had recently been resident in the realm of the King of Alba and had only just returned from a successful campaign to install Edgar, son of Malcolm III, as king there. Edgar was also a friend of Robert's for he had supported Robert and advised him during his attempts to seize the crown of England from his brother, William. In return, Robert had granted him some lands to make him a man. However, a result of the peace deal following the succession war had been that Robert rescind any land he had granted, including that given to Edgar.

Edgar led me towards an isolated spot and we sat down to converse. He asked if I was content on crusade, for he wished to join our expedition and wondered how well he would be treated. I explained how the crusaders respected the brave and the honourable and if he behaved as such, they might not like him but they would respect him and do as he asked. Everybody wanted to survive the crusade and everybody had their reasons for joining. Nobody questioned one another's motives; instead, they all focused on fighting as one and surviving.

In April, a diplomatic mission of brown-skinned, bearded men arrived at our camp. I did not understand their language but it did not seem to be Turkish. We looked around for somebody to interpret their message and Peter the Hermit, who spoke their Arab language, explained these men were diplomats from the Fatimid Caliph in Egypt and wished to speak with our leadership.

They were welcomed, but we were uncertain what dealings we would be having with these Egyptians. One of them addressed me in Greek.

"How much are you being paid?" he asked.

"Nothing," I responded. "I'm here to do God's work."

He began to laugh to himself. "No mercenary is ever doing the work of Allah."

"What mercenary? And who is Allah?" I asked.

"You are the mercenaries and Allah is our all-powerful and all loving creator, who gave his commands to Muhammad. Peace be upon him, as his last prophet."

I was taken aback by this. "I have heard of no such prophet," I stated.

"Muhammad, peace be upon him, lived in these lands four centuries ago. He restored the religion of Allah."

This meant that he would have lived after the time of Jesus. "Why would there need to be more prophets if the Lamb of God, Jesus Christ our Lord, came down to earth?" I asked.

"Jesus, may Allah honour him and grant him peace, was not the son of God, but a prophet," he responded. "He is subordinate to Allah as his creator," he said.

Before we could continue our conversation, the order to escort them to the leadership council was given and they left to meet with our leaders. I was confused as to who these men had been for they did not resemble our previous Turkish foes, but bore a slight resemblance to some of Ridwan and Duqaq's men. Alexander was nearby and I summoned him over.

"Those men, were they Arians?" I asked.

He responded to the contrary, "Those men were Muslims – Shi'ite, I believe, followers of the Fatimid Caliph in Cairo."

This news almost caused me to fall off my seat. "Mahometans? In our camp? Why? Are they not the enemy?" I asked, frantically.

"Relax, Cristo," he responded, seeking to assure me. "Until now, we have fought Sunni Muslims. These Shia hate them more than they hate us, and I will wager my sword and armour that they are trying to reach an agreement for us to aid them in conquering their Sunni enemies."

This was strange news to me. *Mahometans as allies?* I had entered the Holy Land expecting all Mahometans to be barbarous savages who desecrated altars and baptismal fonts. The news that we would, perhaps, have Mahometans allies helping us on our crusade was strange news and challenged everything I had expected from this crusade, I would be grateful for the help, of course. Perhaps we would even become friends with the Mahometans, I had no qualms with befriending a Mahometan, so long as he was not hostile. The Normans had been my enemies in the past and yet I had befriended them, I saw no reason not to extend the hand of friendship to these Mahometans. I intended only to kill those who tried to kill me or who stood in the way of liberating Jerusalem. If they were peaceful, I would count them as close allies and perhaps even close friends.

Everyone was awaiting news of what the talks would produce. We had been weakened somewhat and any reinforcement and any new supplies would be a blessing to us. Perhaps they could even help us capture Antioch and maybe even Jerusalem itself. The Fatimid delegates left the tent and mounted their horses to return to Cairo without speaking a word to anyone. We still had to wait for our leaders to leave the tent and address us. It had not been my turn to guard Robert, but I felt worried about him nonetheless. I had not thought to search them for hidden weapons, as I expected the bodyguards would have done so – and even if they had become hostile, somebody would have raised the alarm. The delegates did not seem to have been involved in any altercation and had no blood on their clothes. I worried our leaders had been covertly butchered though I knew deep down that they were alive and well.

Eventually, they emerged unharmed and Raymond came to address us. "My dear brothers," he began, "I am sure you noticed that we have been visited by envoys from the Fatimid Caliph. We listened to his proposals in good faith; he promised us men, supplies and land if we joined him, a proposal that, though tempting, we were forced to decline."

A collective groan swept the camp as we realised that we were still alone. Raymond sought to quieten us before addressing us again, "My dear brothers, they offered us half of this land we are in to join them, but they would not give us Jerusalem. We courteously told them that we would betray our Lord for no man! We told them that we would fight through a million men on our own if we knew Jerusalem was the end."

Cheering spontaneously broke out at this point.

"We told them that we would rather die fighting alone to reach the land of our Lord and Saviour, Jesus Christ, than to live and never see the Holy City! We will not give in and we will fight until the end! Join us and we will either seize Jerusalem or die trying!"

The camp was now in raptures of cheering and shouts of *"Deus Vult!"*. Many men knelt and prayed. I could not help but feel joy that Raymond and all the leaders were committed to the sanctity of our endeavour. It almost brought a tear to my eye.

Robert later informed me that the Fatimid envoys had refused outright to believe that we were anything other than Byzantine mercenaries and hence had offered us the whole of Syria if we respected their hegemony over Palestine. Going by Byzantine imperial standards, this was apparently a completely acceptable agreement, but this would deprive us of the most important towns: Bethlehem, Nazareth and especially Jerusalem. I could not blame the envoys; they were ignorant of our true purpose. We had explicitly told them, of course, and their ignorance was thus somewhat wilful. They negotiated in good faith for what they believed to be mutual benefit. I respected them for this and was glad that they had been able to part from us with gifts, and had been treated fairly and well during negotiations.

The siege had continued with no real development in the meantime and it was not until May that anything major was to change. In this month, Kerbogha united his forces with those of Ridwan and Duqaq, as well as forces from

Persia and another referred to as Mesopotamia. We were thus forced to brace ourselves for an imminent attack by a vast contingent of hostile Mahometans.

God, however, smiled upon us as Baldwin of Boulogne managed to provide a distraction that delayed the arrival of this force temporarily by diverting their attention to Edessa. We had been granted a reprieve, but we knew that unless we captured Antioch soon, we would be encircled and slaughtered.

Bohemond then revealed the ace up his sleeve. Weeks earlier, he had made contact with an apostate named Firouz from Armenia, who was in control of the tower of the two sisters. Bohemond offered a deal to our leadership; if they agreed to make him Prince of Antioch, he would allow their troops, as well as his, to exploit Firouz's betrayal.

Raymond resisted as best as he could, but he was alone in arguing against the deal and it was accepted without amendment. I felt some sympathy for Bohemond, as well as Raymond. Raymond did not take vows lightly and wished to remain faithful to that which he had made to Alexios – to hand back any former imperial cities captured. However, I had been present when Bohemond had made an agreement for our contingent and he had only promised his support so long as Alexios aided us and we had not sighted Byzantines since the departure of Tatikios some months ago.

On the feast of Pope Eugene I, Count Étienne-Henri of Blois deserted us. I had seen him leave the camp under cover of darkness. It was disconcerting to see a man of such nobility and, until a few months prior, great enthusiasm abandon us. I tried to speak to him, hoping to convince him to stay and remind him how close we were to a breakthrough, but he refused to acknowledge me at all. I would not see him again for some years.

The same day, while patrolling the perimeter, Firouz sent a message requesting Bohemond draw attention away from him by convincing the garrison he was marching to confront Kerbogha, but return at night and scale the walls. I was asked to be among the vanguard sent up the walls on behalf of Robert. Bohemond was to lead us in person and the leadership were anxious that he be adequately protected. My experience as bodyguard to Robert made me a solid choice.

We encountered no resistance on the walls and were able to open the gates and surprise the garrison, who were swiftly overwhelmed before they could adequately respond. Many of our troops perpetrated a massacre of civilians. It was common convention that for eighteen days after the capture of the city, its inhabitants and movable commodities were at the mercy of the victorious besiegers. This did not, therefore, make the massacre moral, but nor did many of them view it as immoral.

The distinction between Muslim and Christian was rather unclear and we discovered later that many of the dead were Christian. Firouz mourned the loss of his brother, a victim of our zealousness. I apologised for what had happened. I had stayed true to my moral decision to kill only those who took up arms against me and so although I was not personally responsible for the deaths of any civilians, I felt somewhat responsible for being too concerned with my mission and not defending the innocent.

When our zeal had calmed down, we were now in

control of the city, but the remnants of the garrison had withdrawn to the citadel and thus the siege was not yet over. Many of us had been swept away by the euphoria of finally capturing Antioch, for it was a most magnificent city. However, our euphoria was to be short-lived as the city held little food due to our efforts during the siege of the city.

Now we were significantly safer within the walls, we were able to scavenge food from the surrounding area. As a result, we were not too disheartened by the lack of food within the city. There was high optimism of our chances of seeing out the siege of Antioch's citadel and life began to seem normal, not in the sense of quotidian but in the sense that we felt safe and were no longer worried we would be imminently slaughtered or sold into slavery.

John the Oxite, a man of the Eastern Church, was installed as patriarch of Antioch in a show of Christian brotherhood. The women of Antioch told us stories of John having been previously hung from the city's walls and his feet beaten by iron rods. It is true that John struggled to walk, but I was unsure if such mistreatment had been the cause or whether the people of Antioch were merely resentful of Mahometan rule.

CHAPTER ELEVEN

On June 4th, I noticed a man trying to unload his cart and joined him in his labour, for he was a man much older than I and he was visibly struggling with the weight. When we had finished unloading the cart, he wiped the sweat off his brow and turned to face me. He said something like "*Shah kay ra*", so I suppose he must have been Persian or, perhaps, Egyptian, for I had come across the Persian "*Shahanshah*" and the Egyptian "*Ra*" in my studies of Greek classics.

When I looked puzzled, he returned my puzzled look with the words "*Eísai Éllinas?*" which means "Are you Greek?". When I responded in the negative – in Greek, of course – he looked more perplexed and inquired how I had come to understand their language for I looked too young to be a mercenary. My birth coincides with the Feast of Saint Apollinaris. I explained to him about my classical education by Raymond and his passing at Dorylaeum. He seemed genuinely upset and remarked that it is sad to lose a friend who is there for you when others are not. He looked downhearted and added something in his own language, "*Orkhada fi Salam?*" and I responded "*pancung*".

I looked towards him and asked "Are you a Mahometan?" to which he seemed taken aback and offended.

"I worship Allah alone. Mahomet – may Allah honour him and grant him peace – is his servant, not our God. We are Moslems, not Mahometans."

I was unsure how to respond to this for I knew little of the beliefs of the Moslems other than their polygamy. I apologised and asked his name. "Khadim Lilkasa" was his response. I told him my name in return. He found it difficult to pronounce and I found his no easier.

We spent a few more hours talking of our lives. I was genuinely intrigued that his life did not seem abnormal. There was no talk of anything evil – no more evil than the happenings I was used to at home, at least. He seemed to be more similar to myself than I would have suspected. We discussed matters of faith for most of this time. Many names of his ancestors were recognisable: Adem, Ibrahim and Musa. He told me of his childhood in the Holy Land and his journeys to Jerusalem. May God deliver us to that Holy City, to visit the religious sites there. These names I did not recognise.

He seemed shocked to hear stories of my homeland. He continuously referred to it as Albion and claimed to have only heard of it in ancient stories. He asked if the land was as cold as they said. I had not considered England particularly cold during my life, but upon my journey east, I found myself having to work hard to adjust to warmer climates. I agreed that by the standards of the Holy Land, England was as cold as ice. He had not encountered snow in his life and he listened to my description with genuine enthusiasm.

When the sun began to set, he invited me into his house to eat. I was uncertain of the protocol for entering the house of a... Muslim and hence I was unsure if it would be best to accept or decline. However, I felt a genuine connection to him, a connection I had only felt with Raymond. As a result, despite my inclinations to reject his invitation, I found myself unable to do so.

When I entered his home, I found it to be of a significantly different design to my own home in England. The architecture was similar but distinct to that I had seen in Constantinople and hence I found it both novel and yet familiar.

Inside were his family: an elderly woman, a couple much older than myself but also much younger than the woman, a young boy and a girl I presumed to be in her teens. At first, they were surprised to see me, but when Khadim introduced me, they began to shout at him. The language was clearly the same as the one Khadim had spoken to me when we first met. Mid-argument, he turned towards me and asked whether I was, or had ever been, a servant of the Greeks or the Armenians? I responded in the negative and Khadim translated for, whom I presume was, his father.

His father became more irate and when Khadim translated again, he appeared to have asked why I had come, if not for the emperor. His father appeared to find the very idea that I had come to protect Christians absurd and incredulous. It quickly became clear to me that neither Khadim nor his family knew that myself and the Greeks were of different rites. When I explained this to Khadim, he seemed bewildered and I was required to give a lengthy explanation – all the while his father was becoming more and more irate.

When the smoke eventually cleared, I was permitted to eat. In line with my Lord's instruction, I took the seat of the lowest prestige. The children offered me their seats, but I refused. The food I ate that day was better than any I had eaten before. It proved highly irritating to my mouth and I was obliged to drink large amounts of water to compensate. I noticed that none of the family were drinking wine or beer and although I was more accustomed to this than water, I did not wish to disobey whatever protocol they were following and made do with water instead.

I left the house late at night. I felt it was an enriching experience to have met these people and to discover how they lived, even if they were not the Christians I had expected to find when I had set out on crusade.

As I returned to camp, I passed Tancred de Hauteville. He was a minor lord and hence was not much removed from us, however he was also the nephew of Bohemond, which gave him a status he, perhaps, ill deserved. Many of the men found it offensive to have to give respect to a man of such little rank. Theoretically, Robert was of a higher rank than either of them, but despite this had submitted himself to Bohemond's judgement. I was, perhaps, the minority; I respected Tancred strongly but this had nothing to do with his status. He was, in fact, an ally. He was on crusade for more genuine motivations than many of the leaders and was, by all accounts, an agreeable figure, hence he had earned my respect and I treated him in high regard.

"Good evening, Cristo," he said to me.

"Good evening, my lord," I responded.

He looked me in the eye. He was of a similar height and age to myself and I found that he related to me because of this. Perhaps he lorded himself over the others in order to compensate for his youth, but with me, because of my own youth, he felt more comfortable and treated me with respect.

"Have you enjoyed your night on the town?" he asked, jokingly.

I chuckled at the suggestion and responded with equal jest. "I fear the alcohol has slowed my body such that I shall not have a hangover for many days."

Tancred's shy smile betrayed the fact he appreciated my humour. He looked beyond me down the street. "This is a lovely city and I can only hope that one day I shall be lord of such a beautiful city and call it my own."

"God willing," I responded.

"Bohemond is highly impressed with you, as is Raymond. If it were up to me, I would entrust you with a fief of your own to govern for I can see you are a reliable and loyal fellow."

"I do not consider myself ready for such an honour," I said, part out of humility and part out of a fear of great responsibility. "It would not be fitting for me to be granted such an honour when others more deserving are with us."

Tancred nodded, understandingly. "But you do want a fief of your own, no?"

I could not say no, for every boy desires to become a man. However, I felt I had done nothing to deserve it. Many of the men I was serving with had been in service to their lord since before I was born and had received no reward. How could I deserve it when I had done barely a year of service?

I greatly resented that we had perpetrated such an

indiscriminate massacre in capturing the city. However, I was physically repulsed to learn the leader of the Moslem resistance to our siege had been captured outside the city and beheaded by a native Christian. I accepted that his rule had turned tyrannous towards the end of it and was greatly resented, especially his expulsion of much of the Christian population prior to the siege. I accepted that by summarily beheading him, the natives were expressing their belief that his crimes condemned him to death.

However, I could not accept the desecration of his body in presenting the head to Bohemond. He would have been more valuable to us alive and that is simply not how one should treat a noble and respectable enemy. I found it wholly detestable and a source of great shame that this was seen as justifiable by my fellow brothers, and worse that Bohemond had not rejected it outright. I never did find out what had been done with the head, but I always hoped it was returned to his son along with the rest of his body.

The fate of his head was of trifling importance by the next day when a watchman was heard screaming. At first, he was too far away to make out with absolute clarity. When I came close enough to hear him correctly, I was sent scrambling for my arms as he continued to shout, "Saracens! Saracens!"

It was Kerbogha of Mosul. It may seem abnormal that any thoughts other than survival entered my head as I prepared for battle, but I found myself praying internally and thanking God for the miracle he had performed. For if we had continued the siege for just three days longer, we would have been trapped and left with the choice of either massacre or surrender. This confirmed one thing to me. We had a weapon the Saracens could never match: the *Godfæder*.

They did not attempt to enter the city on the first day – perhaps they desired to catch us unawares and were put off by our swift response to sighting them. The second day was also quiet, but we were wary of any attempts to exploit our weaknesses, which left our armies in a standoff. By the third day, the standoff was broken.

The order came for them to try to storm the walls. We had been on edge and, as a result, we mobilised far too quickly for them to make an early headway. This was my first experience of defending the walls of a city and I struggled to adapt. It was hard to keep your attention on both those who were scaling the walls and those who had already made it. Luckily, whenever I failed to pay sufficient attention, one of my comrades was able to intervene before our foes were able to exploit my distraction.

One aspect I never forgot about battling on ramparts was that unlike killing a foe with a sword or axe, where death would usually come swiftly, a foe who went over the walls would not meet his end in a few seconds or he might even survive the fall, albeit with fatal injuries. The scream of a man who is facing imminent death he cannot prevent and has time to contemplate is a complex experience to describe. I will never believe I can adequately explain, other than it is less painful than hearing a man crying in agony, unable to get to his feet, and gradually losing his battle for life.

The Saracens made temporary gains on the walls, but were forced to retreat without gaining a foothold. Fighting was fierce and bloody and neither side could have borne the losses for much longer.

The next day was merely a skirmish. Perhaps I am not doing it justice but in comparison to the previous day, it was relatively relaxed. Kerbogha consolidated his position outside the walls on the sixth day and the siege truly began. Many of our men were panicking, as we had not had enough time to gather adequate supplies. It was hard enough to gather enough food for ourselves, never mind the people of Antioch and our resolve was low since we began to starve almost instantly. Escape routes were cut off, the citadel was still being held by Yaghi Sivan's son and there was no chance of reinforcements. We were alone in the world; we would die if we didn't fight and there was a high chance we would die if we did. We needed uplifting.

CHAPTER TWELVE

The next day, a preacher named Peter Bartholomew proclaimed he had received visions of St Andrew, who had promised that the lance that pierced Christ's side on the cross was in the city. He was not alone in this; another proclaimed a vision of Mark the Evangelist, who promised the Saracens would be scattered if the gospel were preached to them from the battlements. Stephen of Valence proclaimed he saw both Jesus and the blessed Virgin, and another, a Scot, proclaimed a vision of St Regulus, who proclaimed the remaining relics of St Andrew were also in the city. Only the vision of St Andrew was taken seriously by the leadership. Raymond was adamant that Peter Bartholomew could be trusted, perhaps because he was one of his subjects, but we were desperate for any sign of divine favour and even this claim would be acceptable.

We were ordered to fast in order to draw closer to God – fasting, however, was barely voluntary by this point since we were already running severely low on supplies. When one fasts, one is supposed to meditate on the passion and suffering of Christ and draw closer to him through one's own suffering. While I was fasting, I began to notice how desperate the plight of the citizens of Antioch was; we were starving, but it looked like many had not eaten since before our arrival. I attempted to pass around some of the food I would not be needing, but the few scraps that could be mustered would hardly have made a major difference to their plight. The only way I could protect their livelihood (including that of Khadim) was to detach Kerbogha from our walls. Jesus had commanded us to feed the hungry, but to do so we would have to go to war.

The decision to obey the commands Peter Bartholomew gave was not unanimously accepted and many believed we had been abandoned by God and must repent in earnest. I didn't care much how we won victory, so long as we did so. I knew we would only win with God on our side, but could not decide whether I truly believed what Peter said or if I was deluding myself with hope. It was alleged that even Adhemar did not believe Peter, pointing out that he had seen the holy lance in Constantinople. I did not know who to believe or what to think.

On June 14th, my mind was made up for me. Peter demanded we dig inside the cathedral and we obliged. Many men dug a hole where Peter requested for a great deal of time and any of us who were free flocked to the dig site. It felt like I was waiting there for all my life. I did not know what to expect. Should I be waiting for a sign? Or should I hope that nothing was found so we could concentrate on the siege?

The diggers eventually gave up and climbed out of the hole without having discovered anything of note. Peter cried out for them to continue but they refused, dejected and disheartened that their hard work had been for naught. Peter, however, merely jumped into the hole and continued frantically digging. This was undoubtedly an interesting and unique spectacle and few left the cathedral, most choosing to see whether Peter was, indeed, a lunatic. Those who left were to miss the most important part of our crusade yet.

Peter gave a shout of triumph and lifted some metal into the air. It was severely rusted and extremely small, but the general outline was that of a spear tip. Some immediately fell to their knees and prayed. I reluctantly followed. I did not know whether I believed this was truly the holy lance, but I knew something far more important. Whatever it was Peter Bartholomew had discovered had given us hope, and we were more determined than ever to defeat the Saracens and march onto the Holy Land. We spent the next two weeks fasting and praying for victory in the upcoming battle.

Despite our hunger, we were more vigorous than before. We believed, once more, that victory was in our grasp. June 28th was to be our do-or-die moment, a battle in which we no longer believed we would die.

Overall command had been ceded to Bohemond for the battle. His resolute defence at Dorylaeum made him the obvious and clear choice. We were fighting for our lives and the men believed that only Bohemond could adequately lead us. If someone else had been chosen, I fear we would have had a riot on our hands. Bohemond divided us into echelons so that we could attack with more mobility. He also arranged us so that we would have maximum protection from the nearby river. I was assigned to the first division to leave the city walls.

When we exited the gate and saw the size of Kerbogha's

army, many were struck with fear. As the first to leave the safety of the walls, we were vulnerable – had he charged towards us, we would have been helpless. However, he waited and waited, and soon our whole force was outside the gates. He did not charge at us; in fact, he began to retreat towards the river, which gave us time to arrange ourselves into the echelons Bohemond desired. I was sent onto the left wing, a decision I later came to regret since the river was to our right and we were thus exposed on our flank. Now was the time Kerbogha made his attack. Despite our exposure, we knew we could not afford to break rank, as to do so would leave the rest of the army vulnerable and a retreat could easily become a rout.

Bohemond, however, then showed exactly why he had been given command. He organised a division from the men available and reinforced our position. Kerbogha's men shattered before the charge and were forced back, for now our line was holding steady. Kerbogha then appeared to become afraid as he set fire to the grass that divided our forces, most likely to deter our forces from attacking his position.

We knew Kerbogha wanted us to remain where we were and thus we rode out to meet his forces. I knew when I signed up for the crusade that I would have to go through hell and charging through the flames made it clear I had done exactly this. Many later claimed that Saint George and Saint Demetrius were marching with us, but I never saw them. However, one of the men who was at my side during the charge appeared like the images I had seen of Saint Maurice.

When we hit their lines, what can only be described as a

miracle occurred. Their entire line was shattered almost in an instant; men began fleeing the battlefield in disarray and the more the line began to break, the more men began to abandon the field. We had fought overwhelming odds and had crushed our opponents. There were only two words to explain this, "*Deus Vult*".

Not long after we returned to the city, we received even greater news: the citadel had surrendered. Antioch was completely ours. Allegedly, as soon as the defenders saw Kerbogha's men crumble before us, they began to beg for terms. Bohemond had demanded the city as his own and the leaders had agreed. The citadel had been personally surrendered to him by Ahmed Ibn Merwan and thus I could see no reason to deny it to him. We had promised the emperor that we would return any former imperial territory so long as he helped us – what was wrong with Bohemond holding Antioch as an imperial fief? Even if I disliked Bohemond, I could not deny him the city. He had been promised it.

The next few months were to pass without much incident, until the month I celebrated my nineteenth birthday and realised that I was no longer a mere child. By my age, Caesar Augustus had been made consul and, despite all I had done, I had yet to accomplish anything of real note. All knights must fight bravely, but what had I done that made me special?

In August, we received news that broke hearts. An outbreak of typhus claimed the lives of many and on August 1st it claimed the life of Adhemar of Le Puy, the man who had comforted me upon Raymond's death. He had been a most pious man on crusade; whenever we risked straying from the path of God, he was there to guide us. Whenever the leaders had proved obstinate or we had been divided by policy, he was there to mediate and reconcile. It was a most humbling experience to hear the preaching of a papal legate on crusade and I would miss him greatly, both for who he was as a man and also since we had lost one of our finest leaders with his death. With the death of the appointed legate, an epistle was sent to Pope Urban II asking him to take direct control of Antioch but he declined, arguing it was in our best interests, and the interests of the church and faith, that we administer it ourselves.

The rest of our year was spent consolidating our gains around Antioch. With Kerbogha's retreat, we were once more able to forage the surrounding countryside for food. We ran into some resistance, however, as many Muslim peasants refused to share food with us. I thus appreciated Khadim's hospitality even more, and we knew that we were unwelcome and undesired here. Khadim, however, proved to be our intercessor. When I complained to him that many peasants were treating us with disdain, he left the city and returned with many supplies that we were permitted to put in the granary, though I gave him some of my share to thank him.

Before this, our starvation had hit critical levels as many of the lesser knights were not receiving enough food. This was the official justification for their mutiny. I noted they were all members of Raymond's contingent. In November, Raymond agreed to placate his mutinous troops and an agreement was made that we would continue our march at the end of 1099. It looked like our fortunes had turned for the better; we had gathered more supplies and were prepared for the long journey ahead. When the map of our route was unfolded, I stood in awe. We would march past Nazareth and Bethlehem and, more importantly, our ultimate destination, Jerusalem.

CHAPTER THIRTEEN

Our march got off to an inauspicious start as Bohemond disappeared from our army and returned to Antioch. He would not rejoin us on our march and I was greatly disappointed at his choice to abandon us. My anger at Bohemond, however, was tempered by allegations of a disgusting crime, committed in the town of Ma'arrat al-Numan. I knew full well our men were desperate for food and there was little we could do about it other than scavenge or capture cities with ample supplies. This meant I had been fully in favour of beginning the siege. It is, however, impossible to defend their actions and I can only hope that their frustration at their inability to capture the city and their worsening starvation had gotten the better of them, or else they had lost all their humanity. I believe that I will go to my grave not knowing what drove them to do as they did. I have believed all my life and been taught that all things are forgivable, yet I do not know how it is possible to forgive them. Surely when one has sunk to the depths of depravity, they cannot repent or turn away from sin. Could paradise truly contain cannibals?

Khadim had asked to join us on our march. He feared for Antioch under Bohemond's rule and hoped that by joining me on campaign, he could find a safer place for his family to live. It was clearly a difficult decision to reach and he feared for his family. His parents were too old and his siblings too young to defend themselves. Without him, they were vulnerable, but he knew he had to leave them temporarily in order to protect them.

It was difficult to convince Robert that Khadim should be permitted to join us. Some feared he was a spy or would betray us. Both Tancred and Robert had sworn fealty to Raymond in the meantime and he was thus restricted in his ability to make an independent decision.

I never told Khadim this, but I promised them that if he turned on us, I would kill him myself. Robert eventually consented to Khadim joining us as my retainer. His role was virtually honorary and he was given no status in our forces. He was to be my responsibility completely. I had noted that Khadim was a man older than myself, but not too much older. When we left Antioch, he looked haggard and worried. I had set off on crusade with the expectation that I would not live to see the end of it. I had nothing to lose. Khadim, however, had people depending on him and he could ill-afford to risk his life like I did.

Our victory at Antioch had clearly driven fear into the hearts of the local elite for we encountered little resistance on our march down the coast. Indeed, whereas the peasants outside Antioch had actively denied us food, the magnates we encountered were more than willing to give us supplies. I suppose this was more out of self-preservation than charity; if so, they were highly astute as those who helped us were left alone, whereas those who chose to fight were attacked.

The leading magnates had, by this time, taken to walking barefoot and dressing as pilgrims. I admit I was jealous of this for I did not feel like a pilgrim considering my arms. However, Robert's safety was my responsibility and I could not, and would not, abandon my responsibilities. Their choice to take on the guise of pilgrims made things harder, however. They were less well protected, which meant we had to take extra precautions, and without weapons, they were unable to join us in our assaults or even come close to the walls, meaning our commanders were often less experienced and more hesitant.

Raymond had marched off to besiege Arqa, allegedly out of jealousy that Bohemond, his social inferior, had established a principality and yet he had not. Meanwhile, the rest of us met at Lattakia and marched southwards in February. We met up with Raymond in March. The siege was proving lengthy and even our arrival did not change matters.

Our failure to bring the siege to an end exacerbated tensions within our camp, even the clergy were divided. Without Adhemar to unite them and restrain tensions, the divide between those who believed in Peter Bartholomew and those who did not widened. The accusations of fraud eventually forced Peter to submit to an ordeal by fire. On the line was not just the veracity of Peter's claims, but also the legitimacy of Raymond his patron. Raymond may have been the most prestigious leader still on crusade, but he was not the inevitable leader. If Peter survived the ordeal, then there could be no argument that Raymond was divinely ordained to be the leader. If not, there would be room for challenges to his authority. Since both Tancred and Robert had sworn fealty to Raymond, it was highly unlikely they would be able to mount a serious challenge to his authority; on the other hand, Godfrey of Bouillon was still independent and was agitated to take control of our forces. Peter emerged from the flames clutching the holy lance, but collapsed to the floor with effort. Debate raged as Peter was left to recover. There were those who argued his grievous wounds proved that he was a fraud. His supporters pointed out that he had survived the ordeal. The eventual outcome was clear, however. Peter died of his wounds a few days later. The holy lance was therefore clearly a fake.

We continued the siege, but since it was seen by many as being a private enterprise for Raymond and not necessary for our advancement, we eventually broke off on May 13th without having made major headway or accomplishing anything of note. A Fatimid embassy then arrived in our camp. The diplomats were sterner than the previous embassy.

They announced that they had captured Jerusalem and wished to make an alliance with us on condition that we advance no further. It appeared that the Fatimids could not understand why we had ventured so far. Though a tactical alliance would be beneficial, it would be simply unacceptable to have marched so far and accomplished so little.

Not even a single holy site outside Antioch had been brought under our control. They could not understand why we were so obstinate and continued to send them away in disgrace and we could not understand how they could not realise why we were here. The Fatimids parted by stating that our obstinacy would cost the Christians of Jerusalem. I knew that rejecting the peace was the best move, although I felt selfish for thinking so, since our choice to advance onwards would lead to hardship for our Christian brethren in Jerusalem. I could only hope that we would make it worth their pain.

We were still a rather large distance from Jerusalem and as a result we did not stay still for very long, often sleeping little and spending hours on the move without rest. When we came to Tripoli, we received a warm welcome and the greatest news available to us, the local lord was an avowed enemy of the Fatimids. As soon as he heard we were intending to besiege Jerusalem, he provided us with fresh horses and a large amount of money with which to buy siege equipment.

It was even alleged that he swore to convert to Christianity if we were successful. Alexander was a major proponent of this rumour, but in private he confided that he spread it to quell the fears of men who believed that once we had won victory, we would be outnumbered and outflanked by hostile Muslims. Rumours of a friendly and powerful convert would do wonders for their morale. I did not know what to do about this; it was morally unacceptable to lie, for good can never come out of an evil act, but if I revealed that the story was fictitious then the men might lose hope.

I kept quiet but internally I was morally tormented. This revelation also led me to a more important question, that of what I would do once the crusade was over. I had been so focused on the crusade itself that I had not really considered what I would do once it was finished. Every boy wanted land so that he could become a man, but could I really make a life here in the Holy Land and leave behind my home? It was a veritable dilemma.

I was not the boy I once was. When I had set out, I was a beardless youth, but as I pondered this question I began to stroke my facial adornment. At first I had let my beard grow, as I lacked the time and resources to shave. It was not unusual for a Saxon to have a moustache, but they were much less common among the Normans. Beards, however, were a veritable rarity for me. At first I was apprehensive at the prospect of growing a beard since I wondered how it would be received. I realised soon afterwards that many of the men in the Holy Land had beards and though I received some strange glances, many paid little attention as the time and ability to maintain a clean-shaven face was becoming more and more impossible.

As we continued our march, we passed Beirut and then Tyre, but then turned inland at Jaffa. When we reached Ramlah, we found it unoccupied. Due to its relative proximity to Jerusalem, we decided to make Ramlah our first conquest of the state we were to found. We appointed a bishop of Ramlah-Lydda for the church of Saint George. It was considered particularly ominous that the first church we captured in the vicinity of Jerusalem was dedicated to one of the saints who had helped us at Antioch. Many of the Aragonese and Genoese men celebrated wildly, since Saint George was their patron. The more I heard of him, the more interested in his cult I became and I hoped that devotion to him would spread to England.

June 6th was a particularly important date since it was the day Tancred raised his banner over the church of the nativity in Bethlehem, though the next day would be the most important day of all.

June 7th 1099 – a day I could never forget, for it was the day I first caught sight of the most holy city of Jerusalem. The culmination of all my expectations and hopes. When I first caught sight of the city, I was reduced to tears, as were many of my comrades. A whole host fell to their knees and prayed, myself and Alexander included. Khadim saw that I was overwhelmed and when I was finished praying, he put his arms around me to comfort me. I simply could not control my emotions.

I should have died and yet I was here, ready to storm the walls and enter the city that the Lord God had walked only a millennia ago. My heart pounded with anticipation and excitement at what would soon happen. It was now within our grasp and I was more eager than ever to capture the city. Many had dreamed about what I was now living through. I was twenty years old and I had accomplished the goal of a lifetime.

Without Bohemond's men, we were severely short in numbers and the prospect of a lengthy siege like that conducted at Antioch was untenable. As a result, we sought to take the city by assault as soon as we were sufficiently organised to do so. Our assault was given a further expediency by the fact the local governor had prepared for our arrival by stripping the surrounding countryside of food supplies and poisoning all the wells. Worse still, the Fatimid envoy's threat to make life difficult for the Christians in Jerusalem was proven to be true when we discovered what must have been the entire Christian population of Jerusalem scouring the countryside for food and water like us, claiming they had been expelled on the pretext that their loyalty was suspect.

When we eventually made our first assault on the garrison, I was assigned to attack the north walls, the reason being that by this point, Robert had defected from Raymond to Godfrey. Thus I was obliged to submit to his authority and our encampment was sited alongside Godfrey's not Raymond's. The debacle over Peter Bartholomew had obviously taken its toll on his legitimacy as leader. Nevertheless, we were to be the main force for the assault with Raymond's men being a distraction. This was obviously highly prestigious but since our numbers had dwindled – there cannot have been more than 2000 knights left – we were stretched very thin and had to cover large amounts of wall. We fought valiantly and I did my utmost to push on towards the Tower of David, believing if we could seize such an important fortification, the men would be reinvigorated. However, we could not push far enough and we eventually withdrew without making any headway.

Our desperate situation meant we suffered many losses, but also struck a blow to the garrison. It was clear that they were too afraid to seek to dislodge us themselves and only desired to hold out until they could be relieved. This meant that though they were fresher than us, they did not fight with much determination, nor were they particularly experienced. My time on crusade had made me battle-hardened and, as a result, I was able to swiftly bring down anyone brave enough to engage me in a duel. We may not have made a breakthrough, but it was clear that the defenders were scared and I knew we could take advantage of this.

By the grace of God, two Genoese galleys arrived at Jaffa

soon after our assault and provided much-needed supplies. They could not bring enough to keep us supplied for long, but we were grateful for the succour. In a meeting of the remaining three leaders, it was decided a common purse for the construction of siege engines should be created. My contribution was mostly symbolic, but I felt obligated to donate nonetheless.

Wood also began to be gathered from Samaria in order to construct these engines. We did not receive a particularly warm welcome from the residents and I was unsure whether the gospels should have taught me to expect this or whether I should have been surprised by it.

By June, we were once again low on water and Khadim was panicking about finding clean water with which to make his ablutions. At first, I felt his fears were unjustified, but as I thought about it and watched his behaviour, I realised how serious this was to him and how I would feel the same way if I had been unable to hear mass. I therefore gave up some more of my water ration to permit him to make his ablutions.

Further grim tidings came from the locals in June when they indicated that the local governor had summoned reinforcements prior to our arrival and we would, once again, be threatened with being trapped between the walls and a relief army, which was marching towards us. Realising that our situation was now more desperate, the decision to dismantle the Genoese galleys was taken, in order that we could build further siege towers. The wood we gathered from Samaria had been enough to build two siege towers, a battering ram and some catapults, but this was insufficient since the key to Jerusalem lay in seizing the walls. We were more numerous and experienced than the garrison, but could not make our superiority count until we had breached the walls.

The night before the assault, Khadim was tending to my wounds and began asking me what I expected would happen tomorrow. I was obviously eternally hopeful that we could seize the city with minimal casualties and then defeat the Fatimid relief force, if it ever arrived.

I asked him how he felt that I was up against his religious brethren, but he told me that the Fatimids were not his brothers. He denounced them as heretics and Kafir's. Khadim spoke of how he was looking forward to visiting Jerusalem and kept mentioning something called the Al-Aqsa Mosque. I found it rather strange since he lived so close to Jerusalem, but he claimed that he did not have the time to visit and had not done so for many years. When I asked what his plans were when I had completed my vow, he contorted his face in a manner I believe meant he was slightly disappointed. I had been enjoying his company and it appears he enjoyed mine. I knew that we would have to go our separate ways once the crusade was over and I was at peace with the fact I would have to leave him behind – indeed, I had realised as much about both Raymond, may he rest in peace, and Alexander.

Though I suppose he had not given much thought to it. "I suppose I may settle down in Jerusalem with my family if the situation is favourable," he responded.

"And if not?" I enquired.

"Then I suppose I will have to return to Antioch and hope Bohemond is a fair ruler," he said. "What sort of ruler will he be?"

I thought about my response. Bohemond had shown himself to be both ruthless and cunning, but also courageous and honourable. I could neither completely denounce him nor praise him, and sought to find a middle ground that would not cause Khadim alarm nor leave him unprepared for the problems he was likely to encounter under Bohemond's rule. After taking some time to carefully craft my words, I responded, "If you had asked me before my venture, I would have said he was a greedy and vicious ruler, but he has shown himself to be a worthy and chivalrous commander. He is no saint but nor is he a demon. He is a worldly ruler and I can say little more with certainty."

Khadim understood. Bohemond was not going to be the perfect ruler, but Khadim believed that he would be a less arbitrary ruler than his predecessor in Antioch. I hoped that the best would come out of Bohemond, but I feared that his victory would only make him more rapacious.

I received another letter from my cousin, informing me that his enemy, Earl Hugh of Shrewsbury, had died in battle and he had been able to return home to recover his patrimony without any resistance. My last letter had been written during the siege at Antioch and he had expressed his belief that my fortunes would improve just as his own had. He promised me a place at his court and some land in the far north if I so desired. A courtier who had been a crusader would be a valuable asset even more so since I was a relative. Nevertheless, I knew nothing of the land and could not speak the language. I would likely visit him once the crusade was over, but I saw no reason to settle there.

CHAPTER FOURTEEN

The night of June 14th was when we began our assault. Prior to this we had heard mass and prayed for success, and that we would all survive. The walls of Jerusalem were a terrifying obstacle, but we had not come so far to turn back now.

As I said goodbye to Khadim, he grabbed my arm, "May you win victory today, insh'allah. When this war is over, I hope to live in peace with my family. When my siblings are of age, I shall marry and start my own family. When first I heard about your so-called crusade, I was afraid, but I now see that in the midst of all this deceit and dishonour, there are still those who are fair and compassionate – for this, I thank you, Cristo." His gratitude was touching and I knew that it was true and heartfelt.

"Peace be with you," I said as I kissed him.

"And with you, Cristo," he responded.

We had only two siege towers, but we knew that one would be enough. If we could get men on the walls, then they could open the gates and the city would be ours. Due to the fact I was not proficient in archery, there was very little I could do until a siege tower had reached the walls. My armour was primarily intended to try and soak up the fire to give our siege engines time.

The Fatimids mounted a passionate defence, throwing anything and everything at us. Midway through the battle, we received news that the tower attacking the south section of the wall had gone up in flames and if we could not protect our tower, the siege would be hopeless. Therefore, we spread out and tried to goad the defenders into focusing their fire on us instead of the siege tower. It was an anxious wait and many gave their lives deflecting attention away from the tower. For two hours, we waited for contact with the walls. When the contact finally came, the sense of relief was indescribable. We finally had men on the walls.

Since the tower was under the command of Godfrey, his men were given priority to climb onto the walls and Robert's men, myself included, were obliged to wait for the gate to open. I had expected a long wait but the fighting proved short, with men already on the walls. The Fatimids were terrified and quickly retreated. When I finally entered the city, I was expecting to have to sweep up the remnants of the garrison, but I turned out to be wrong. The garrison had completely collapsed and we had free rein of the city. Without anyone to fight, I was unsure what I should be doing. I presumed we would begin preparations to seize the citadel, but what I experienced sent shivers down my spine and into my very soul.

It was a custom in Europe that once a city had fallen, it was at the mercy of the besiegers who were able to do with it as they pleased. Generally, this amounted to pillage and, among the more sexually rapacious, potentially rape. It was a normal part of our warfare. In Jerusalem, however, there was almost no pillage nor was there much rape, but there was wholesale murder and slaughter, so much so that my ankles were stained with blood. I saw bodies of men, women and children cut down, disembowelled and beheaded – a most distressing sight. These were innocent people, unarmed and no threat to us. There was no reason to deprive them of their right to life.

I walked around the streets in a state of shock. I felt like these events were not real and I moved around like a spirit among mortal men, unable to be seen or heard or affect what was going on around me. Eventually, I met Tancred in the street. He looked almost as traumatised as I, carrying his standard as if he was at the forefront of a funeral march. He looked into my eyes.

"This is not what I intended, Cristo," he stated.

"This is not right," I responded.

"We must stop this, but how?" he asked.

His standard was recognisable to even the least intelligent of our number and I convinced him to hand it over to a group of citizens who had sought refuge on the roof of the holy temple. Tancred was a member of the de Hauteville house and to harm those who bore his standard would be unacceptable. They would, therefore, now be safe.

Unable to comprehend what I had witnessed, I made headway for the Holy Sepulchre so that I could pray for the end of this atrocity. As I knelt down and began praying, I began to weep. I know not whether it was because of the fact I had succeeded and was now praying at the site of our Lord's very death and resurrection, or whether it was in sorrow for those who had been massacred around me. The church had always taught me that the Lord had a plan for me and my life, and that everything happens for a reason, but I simply could not understand why God would let this happen or what it would accomplish. I cried out to him in anguish and then remembered the story of Job and realised that it was futile. I finished my prayers and exited the church.

As I passed through the streets once more, I noticed a fresh group of bodies. As I drew closer, I noticed that underneath them was Tancred's banner. The murderers respected neither the family honour of the de Hautevilles nor the sanctity of life. When Tancred was informed that his banner had been cast to the ground and disrespected, he was furious. He admonished his men for their part in the massacre and when I returned to Robert's camp, I did the same to my comrades. Considering I was their equal and not their superior, I was surprised to note that they showed me respect and did not attack me. What I said was disrespectful, but I was passionate about the sanctity of life and greatly angered by what had transpired.

Now that the city had fallen, we would need to decide upon its administration. Somebody would have to take charge and there were debates as to who merited the honour. I was in favour of Jerusalem becoming a papal fief but since the death of Adhemar, we lacked strong papal representation in our ranks – his successor, Daimbert, didn't have the popularity and respect Adhemar had enjoyed. Hence, despite being papal legate, he failed to be elected patriarch of Jerusalem.

There were arguments that Raymond, as the richest and most prestigious lord among us, should be handed the city, but he refused to accept any title whatsoever. Godfrey as the de facto leader of our enterprise after the departure of Bohemond had the strongest claim, however, and indeed it was he who was given control of the city a week after its capture. In a humble move I greatly appreciated, he refused a crown or the title "King of Jerusalem" stating that it would be wrong to be called "king" and wear a crown of gold, where the King of Kings had worn a crown of thorns.

With the Holy Sepulchre now under our control, we also needed to elect a patriarch. The popular candidate was Arnulf of Chocques, but since he was an enemy of Peter Bartholomew, Raymond spoke vehemently against him and it was only when he departed on pilgrimage that Arnulf was finally elected. Four days after his election, on August 5th, he discovered the relic of the true cross and there were wild celebrations. Godfrey even promised to carry the cross in the imminent battle against the Fatimid relief force, which was approaching.

However, it was not all good news. With Jerusalem now captured, Khadim decided to return to Antioch. He intended to stay in Jerusalem for a while longer and gather mementoes from the Al-Aqsa Mosque and the dome of the rock before returning. I promised to visit him on my route back to England and anytime I returned on pilgrimage. He promised he would tell his children of my honesty and valour even if I was not a Muslim and I promised I would say the same of him to my children. I then bade him goodbye and he began marching towards Antioch.

CHAPTER FIFTEEN

Six days later, we arrived at Ascalon and met with the Fatimids. They numbered at least 20,000 and we numbered just over 10,000, and yet we had cause to be optimistic since even a defeat would not be catastrophic as we could retreat to Jerusalem's walls. A victory, however, would ensure the safety of Jerusalem. It had been a long time since we entered a battle where our entire survival was not at stake and we were still joyous from our capture of Jerusalem and the discovery of the Holy Cross. Our motivation made us a formidable force.

When we arrived, we discovered animals grazing outside the city walls. Men captured in a skirmish near Ramla alleged that they had been deliberately placed outside the city in the hope it would encourage ill-discipline among our ranks and allow the Fatimids to attack us while we were pillaging the area, thereby making us easier to defeat.

Since they were surprised at Ramla, we believed that the Fatimids were not yet aware of our arrival in the area. As it turned out, we were able to turn the Fatimid's tactics against them. By having the animals march alongside us, we were able to give the appearance that we were more numerous than we really were.

The next morning, we discovered the Fatimid encampment and prepared to attack. We divided ourselves into nine divisions of which Robert was to make up the centre. When we hit the camp, we caught the Fatimids by surprise. They fought valiantly, but by the time they were ready for battle their losses were catastrophic. The Fatimids were much less armoured than us and when Robert commanded us to charge, they collapsed like a burning straw hut.

I cannot tell how many I felled that day, but line after line of infantry collapsed under our charge and when the heavy cavalry joined the battle, I felled at least ten. I estimate at least one hundred men fell by my sword in the battle.

The heavy cavalry was the final gambit of the Fatimids and when they failed to stave us off, panic spread throughout their lines. Their commander hurriedly retreated back to the city. In their panic, some ran into the sea and others climbed trees in the hope of escaping us, only to be killed by our archers. Worst of all, many were trampled while trying to retreat into the city.

When the Fatimids had all retreated or been killed, we captured their now-abandoned camp and waited for them to sally forth. When morning came, we discovered that the Fatimids were abandoning Ascalon and retreating back to Egypt. With no attack forthcoming, we plundered their camp and seized the standard and the commander's tent before setting the remnants alight.

We arrived back in Jerusalem the next day. A minor dispute arose between Godfrey and Raymond over who should be allowed to take possession of Ascalon, despite the fact the city had not yet surrendered, which hardened the resolve of the defenders. In the end, the dispute was resolved when so many of our comrades returned home that we no longer had enough knights to continue a siege. I could understand their decision to return home since they had fulfilled their vows. Even though I wished they would stay on, I knew it would be asking them to endure further hardship.

Now that Jerusalem had been cleared of bodies and wreckage from the siege, I was able to walk through the streets and experience the wonders of the city. The Al-Aqsa Mosque and the Dome of the Rock were being converted into churches and Christians were coming from across the Holy Land and even as far as Hungary in order to settle in Jerusalem.

Markets had been set up with many exotic wares, as well as relics for sale. Silk and spice, both of which were rare commodities back home, were readily available and much more affordable. Godfrey had begun to institute a currency for his new realm that was based on the Islamic dinar coins in circulation in the region.

The coat of arms of the kingdom began to be erected around the city. It was quite a bizarre mix since it contained a cross d'or and field d'argent, though I suppose this enhanced the prestige of the kingdom due to its unique design.

Although I had visited the Holy Sepulchre, I decided that I should walk the Via Dolorosa and trace the footsteps of the passion of our Saviour, beginning at the garden of Gethsemane before moving south to Mount Zion, where the house of Caiaphas the high priest was located. Circling the temple mount to the site of the praetorium, I headed back towards the Holy Sepulchre.

There was a large divide between the Christians who held the churches on the western hill of Jerusalem and those who held churches on the eastern hill where the praetorium, where Jesus stood trial before Pilate, was located. Each claimed that it was in the vicinity of their own churches. I chose to take the path of the western churches since it was the traditional route and this led me to Mount Zion. The Sepulchre was not actually a particularly large or spectacular building since its eastern section was actually in ruins. The value of the site lay in its religious significance, not in spectacular architecture; indeed, underneath the basilica was a cistern known as "the chapel of the invention of the cross" since it is where St Helena, the mother of Emperor Constantine, discovered the true cross we had found earlier on our crusade, as well as being the site of Jesus' burial.

As I walked the streets still awash with joy and fervour at having visited the tomb of our Saviour and walked the route of his passion, I noticed four lightly armoured men were accosting one of the locals. As I approached, I noticed that one of the men was Alexander.

They had been pushing him around and hurling religious abuse regarding his Islamic faith. When one of them attempted to seize a book he was carrying, he retaliated and a short brawl broke out. Surprised, I attempted to intervene, but before I reached them Alexander drew his sword and ran it through the unfortunate man.

I arrived just as he withdrew his sword, both in shock at what had happened and anger that I had failed to save his life. I knocked Alexander to the ground with a powerful punch and even drew blood. Surprised, his accomplices scattered and Alexander was left alone and confused. When he came to his senses, he wiped the blood from his mouth and angrily asked me why I had attacked him. His strange method of speaking indicated I may have inflicted more damage than I had realised. Annoyed, I responded in kind and condemned his attack on an unarmed man. He was obstinate that since he was a Muslim what he did was not sinful and denounced me as an apostate for standing up for a Muslim. When I stood my ground, he backed off, likely fearing a confrontation. I disagreed with his assertion that violence against innocent Muslims was justified, but he was intelligent enough to realise he could not hope to justify attacking another crusader. He then walked away and I turned to check on the victim. When I saw his face, I was filled with dread.

Khadim lay dead before me. I checked his body as best as I could in the hope I could find any sign that he was still alive, but to my sadness, I could find none. I kept trying in the hope I was mistaken, but no matter how hard I tried, I could not do anything. Helpless, I fell to my knees and prayed for his immortal soul. When I had finished commending his soul to the Lord, I picked up his body and carried it to Robert's quarters. I knew it would be almost impossible to have Alexander and his men put on trial for the murder, but if I could not ensure justice for Khadim, I would, at least, ensure he received an honourable burial.

When I arrived at his quarters, the guards were shocked to see me carrying a dead body. I do not believe they would have stopped me even if I had not been carrying Khadim, since I had often acted as bodyguard for Robert. They stepped aside and let me pass into his quarters.

When I entered, Robert seemed taken aback and almost fell over in surprise. I told him that now I had secured our position in Jerusalem, I would be leaving the city immediately. Robert stated that he was making preparations to return to Normandy, but I said that I desired to return on my own and in my own time. He agreed to my proposition and gave me permission to leave his service. Now released from my obligations to Robert, I washed and mended Khadim's wounds, before securing him to my horse and beginning the journey to Antioch.

When I arrived, I took his body straight to his family. I ensured that I did not let his family see his body until his younger siblings were out of the way. His mother wailed at the sight of her dead son and his father looked at me angrily. I knelt before him and lowered my head in submission. If he wished to punish me, I deserved it for failing his son. If he had killed me, I would not have blamed him, but instead he placed his hand gently on my head. I knew he wanted to do me harm and in the same position I am not sure I could have suppressed my anger. He chose to forgive me and I am grateful for his mercy – it is more than was deserved.

I left his house soon after, since it was their custom that his closest male relatives should ritually cleanse him in preparation for his burial. In the meantime, I went to find some cloth with which he could be covered. I had taught Khadim some Saxon words during our friendship and he, in turn, had taught me some Arabic, which allowed me to grunt basic words at his father and understand the basics of what he was asking me to do.

The merchants, however, spoke excellent Greek, which made shopping for the cloth significantly easier. I was even able to ask them for advice on what sort of cloth I should buy. The shroud was to be simple and modest, made out of only three pieces of cloth. I eventually purchased a shroud of white cotton with which to cover him.

When I returned, some of his family had gathered to pay their respects. This continued for a few hours after he had been enshroud. When they had finished, they began their funeral prayers. Not knowing what to do, I kept out of the way and silently said my own prayers. There were many prayers that needed to be said according to their religious law, which meant they finished their prayers long after I finished. I had already prayed for his forgiveness, which brought me comfort.

Strangely, there was no coffin and instead he was placed on his right side in the direction of the Qibla in Mecca. Soil was placed under his head, chin and shoulder by his next of kin, who then lowered him into his grave. All present then poured three handfuls of soil into the grave while quoting from their holy book.

More prayers were said and finally gravediggers fully buried him under the supervision of the eldest male relative. It was at this point that I decided to leave, since there were more prayers of forgiveness to be done and a three-day mourning period to be observed by his relatives. In order to ensure modesty, the grave marker would be small, if one was used at all. I marked his grave with my sword, since Khadim had helped me greatly by cleaning my weapons.

As I returned to the city, I was stopped by one of the guards who told me that Bohemond requested my presence. With nothing else to do, I agreed to be escorted to his palace immediately. I did not know what he desired, but nor did I care. I had just lost one of my closest friends and no matter what he had to say, I would still be mourning the loss.

When I received my audience, Bohemond addressed me as "the angelic hero" and that in light of my excellent service while on crusade, he would offer me my own fief in the new principality of Antioch as his vassal. It did not require thought to respond.

Whereas once I would have accepted this offer, like any boy wishing to become a man would have, I could not forget what had happened to Khadim and I was sickened by the massacre at Jerusalem. I did not wish to remain in the service of any of the crusader leaders any longer. I rejected his offer without any hesitation. I stroked my beard and backed out of the room. I left the palace not knowing what I was going to do, but I hoped I could make amends for what we had done in Jerusalem.

With that, I set off into the desert with no direction in mind and completely alone.